KIRK

Gun For Hire Book 3

CHARLENE RADDON

KIRK THE HANGMAN
GUN FOR HIRE, BOOK THREE

Charlene Raddon

Copyright © 2024 by Charlene Raddon
Cover by Charlene Raddon,
www.silversagebookcovers.com

All rights reserved. No part of this publication may be reproduced, distributed or transmitted in any form or by any means, without prior written permission.

Charlene Raddon www.charleneraddon.com
Book cover designed by Charlene Raddon
www.silversagebookcovers.com

This is a work of fiction. Names, characters, places, and incidents are a product of the author's imagination. Locales and public names are sometimes used for atmospheric purposes. Any resemblance to actual people, living or dead, or to businesses, companies, events, institutions, or locales is completely coincidental.

ACKNOWLEDGEMENTS

I want to thank everyone who helped me. I feel so lucky to know such fantastic authors, let alone get them to join my series. I know your books will make this a real winner.

Gratitude also to Kathi Oram Peterson and Maureen Mills for critiquing my work, Linda Broday for all her help setting things up and encouraging me along the way, and my new and brilliant editor, Dianne Rich of DMR Editing.

Last but not least, thanks to my beta readers. You know who you are.

Love you all, ladies

Chapter One

Red River Crossing, Idaho, 1874

Kirk Reddick looked out the window at the crowd gathering in the street. He could only see a bit of the view, the window being on an alley between the marshal's quarters and a tobacco shop. Kirk knew the Red River, which had given the town its name, flowed just out of view. He'd seen it on his way in and figured the water's name and reddish hue came from the red rock formations that bracketed it for some distance. Despite all the people milling about, waiting for the show to begin, he could see part of the mercantile and a dress shop offering alterations.

Shaking his head, he moved from the window to the

dresser, where he paused to smell the marshal's pipe in an ashtray. The scent of pipe smoke reminded him of his father, who commonly had a pipe in his mouth. Sometimes, Kirk entered a tobacco shop just for the smell and the memories. He needed to write his parents. It had been too long, and he couldn't count on his brother, Cage, to keep their folks updated. He smiled slightly, imagining his mother scolding him for putting off writing. Regrettably, he had few pleasant things to talk about these days. In truth, he had none.

Yelling from outside reminded him of his purpose here in Red River Crossing. He didn't want to be here, not for the purpose that had brought him. He hated everything about his job and the residents eagerly yelling for the scheduled event to occur. They made him ill. Everything about his work nauseated him.

The situation resembled a ghoulish circus, except with wooden buildings instead of tents and no stands selling trinkets and food or offering games of chance. Plus, no elephants or clowns. Instead, the entertainment was a hanging.

How sad was that?

A circus wouldn't have gallows, especially like this one, built high enough for everyone to see and provide space for the body to fall through the trapdoor. Similar structures were too often slapped together, barely sufficient to last through the hanging. This one was well-built, with a double door left open in front so people could see the corpse dangling like a deer or other creature waiting to be gutted and skinned—more blood and guts for the audience to see.

Perhaps instead of his black outfit, he should dress as a clown to entertain the children, like the two adolescent boys who ran past the window a second ago. Kirk snorted. Where were the parents? He'd seen small children as well. Why? As a lesson that crime wasn't worthwhile? Surely, children would be badly disturbed by seeing a man executed, causing nightmares and affecting them for much of their lives. Even Kirk found it traumatic. How could people gain pleasure from observing such gory events and yet revile the man who provided the show—the hangman? But they did.

The whole thing was sick, in his estimation. Did these people see no value in life? Every life, whether animal or vegetable, had worth. Whatever time a thief or a killer spent on earth could yield some good. After all, such a man had produced Kirk, who had never robbed or harmed anyone except the men he hanged, and that wasn't by choice. He should write a sermon on the subject, except he was no longer a preacher.

Kirk Reddick was a hangman.

A knock came on the door. "Kirk? It's time."

"Be right there." He turned away from the window, picked up the hood he'd removed while he waited, and pulled it on. He'd had it designed to keep his identity secret from the public and avoid trouble. He'd been cursed, beaten to within an inch of his life, smeared with rotten fruits and vegetables, had dogs sicced on him, been literally chased out of town, and once barely missed being tarred and feathered, as if he had chosen this life. Now, he disguised himself by wearing an all-black costume and a hood with only eye holes to hide behind. It fit just loose enough to allow him to do up the buttons on one side.

Kirk appreciated his old friend, Russell Sandford, letting him use his private room behind his office. Such favors came rarely. After his last hanging, he'd bought a tinker's wagon that allowed him to change into his costume unseen. After the hanging, he'd quickly hide in his tiny new home, change into regular clothing, and drive away. It waited now in an alley behind the jail. He'd be able to leave the moment he completed his job. If no one knew what he looked like, they wouldn't be able to find and torment him. He considered it a true blessing.

After a final check in the mirror to ensure he'd put the hood on correctly, Kirk opened the door, strode down the hall, and entered the office.

The prisoner, Sam Dunstan, a stumpy man with a jutting jaw that gave him the look of a two-legged hippo, looked over at him while Russsell cuffed his hands behind his back. "So, this is the man who's going to string me up, is it?" the prisoner quipped. "What's the costume for? You going to a ball after you hang me?" He gave a phony laugh.

Kirk walked to the door, ignoring the man.

"Wait," Dunstan said. "You're going to end my life today, yet I don't know you from Adam. Doesn't it bother you, killing men who've done you no wrong?"

Kirk paused. Was the man serious? "I'm just doing my job."

Dunstan snarled an ugly oath, questioning the legality of his birth. Kirk ignored him.

"Come on." Russell pushed the prisoner toward the door.

With a sigh, Kirk followed after a few moments, giving them time to climb to the top of the scaffold. But when he went out, Russell still stood by the gallows stairs, trying to get Dunstan to climb them. The prisoner had gotten cold feet. Not surprising. Kirk had seen it numerous times before.

"Go on, get up there. Or do you want me to end it here with a bullet to your brain?" The marshal drew his six-shooter and shoved it into the man's back

"Yeah," Dunstan answered. "Do it. It would be more pleasant." But he climbed the stairs, Russell behind him.

Kirk came last, his steps slow and reluctant. A few people nearby noticed him and stepped away, alarm in their eyes. He heard their comments.

"Who the devil is the big guy in the black?"

"The hangman, of course, ya idget."

"Adele, did you see him?" a woman asked. "He's scary."

Adele answered, "I heard they're taken from the prisons, no better than the men they hang."

"They're worse," the first woman said. "They wouldn't do it if they didn't take pleasure in killing men."

When Kirk reached the top of the six-foot-high platform and became visible to the rest of the crowd, the people booed and threw garbage at him. Nothing new.

He checked the noose, tugging it to test the knot as he always did to ensure a hanging went right. He'd once witnessed an event where the hangman had poorly tied the knot. The victim had kicked, clawed at the rope at his neck, gulped, choked, frothed at the mouth, and gurgled until he had finally suffocated—instead of his neck instantly breaking and killing him as it should have. It had revolted Kirk.

Dunstan stepped into place just when Kirk released the rope. It swung inches from the prisoner's nose. With a gasp, he dropped to his knees and broke into sobs. His bladder released, soaking his pants. The crowd roared with laughter, jeered, and tossed rotten food at him. A tomato splattered against his cheek.

Kirk had seen it a half-dozen times, and as before, it brought out the reverend in him. Unable to bear watching the man, Kirk bent, took Dunstan's arm, and gently hauled him to his feet. "You're all right," Kirk whispered. "It is not this bunch of idiot townspeople you face. Close your eyes and mind to that. Listen only to me. You stand before your Lord. He sees not a thief or a killer of innocents but a beloved son who has strayed from the path of righteousness. Go to Him, let Him lead you home, for He loves you despite your sins. Let Him show you the way to salvation."

"Yes." Dunstan straightened. "I want that. I want to make amends and become a good man. I've been bad for too long. Ma tried to teach me right before she died." More tears came. "I miss her so."

"Then make her proud now, for she'll be watching. Stand strong and prepare to meet your maker with pride and joy, for it is a good thing. See your mother waiting and your other loved ones already there.

"I will put a hood on you now, so you will no longer see those who would defile you but, instead, the Man who awaits you in Heaven. The One who will direct your path from now on. Are you ready?"

Dunstan pulled himself up as tall as possible and straightened his shoulders. "I'm ready."

Kirk slipped the hood over the prisoner's head and gently added the noose so that Dunstan would barely feel it.

Russell read his crime and conviction to the audience. Later, he'd wire Kirk's *keeper*—the judge who arranged this inglorious job for him—to prove Kirk had completed his task. Dunstan was only another sinner he would send to the other side.

"String 'im up," someone in the mob yelled.

"Yeah. What's the hangup? Do it!" came another voice, followed by a chorus of "Do it! Do it! Do it!" and more rotten vegetables.

"He's a killer," a woman cried. "Send the murdering rat to hell."

Was she a housewife? Kirk wondered. A mother? Did she go to church on Sunday? Bah.

Russell tucked the papers away. "Does the condemned have anything to say?"

A rotten apple splattered against Dunstan's pant leg. A second one followed, and he began to shake.

"Hurry up, will ya?" a voice shouted. "Hang him."

Kirk moved just behind Dunstan, near his ear. "Calm yourself and ignore those idiots. They don't know you as God does. He sees inside your heart and knows why you've done the things you've done better than you do."

Dunstan raised his chin.

"Does the prisoner have anything to say?" Marshal Sandford repeated.

"No," Dunstan said firmly.

The marshal nodded to Kirk.

The time had come. Kirk had no way to delay or escape his chore. Regret filled him, as it always did, for taking the life of another human being was a sin.

Integrity and only integrity forced him to pull the trapdoor lever.

It banged open.

Dunstan plummeted.

As always, Kirk listened for the crack of the neck-breaking but heard only the jeers, curses, and laughter from those who watched.

The corpse swung gently now, quiet. Dunstan had gone to meet his maker.

Relieved yet full of guilt, Kirk stepped back. It was over. And his victim hadn't suffered.

How Kirk hated this work. To take a life was wrong. His soul must have turned black long ago with the first hanging he executed. Would he go to hell even though he'd taken this job to save his innocent brother?

A rider on a lathered horse thundered up the street and yelled, "Wait!"

The rider, seeing the carcass slowly dangling, shouted a foul curse, yanked a six-shooter from the gun belt on his hips, aimed and fired, then galloped away.

The bullet creased the side of Kirk's skull. Pain exploded through his brain.

He'd been shot.

He sucked in a breath, and his mouth filled with the cotton hood he wore. He strained to spit it out with a tongue as dry as the Sahara. The world spun. His legs wobbled like wet mud.

He staggered backward, the image of his smiling

brother filling his mind. Then Cage was gone, and Ma appeared, arms outheld. Kirk tried to reach out and hug her, but his body wouldn't cooperate. The platform beneath his feet vanished, and he plunged from the gallows.

Death had finally found him. He'd hung his last man.

As darkness claimed him, Kirk gave a silent, dour cheer.

Chapter Two

Adina Kinnaird stepped from the newspaper office where she worked part-time to see what all the yelling was about outside. Men stood on the gallows erected in front of the jail and almost before the newspaper office. On the far side, a crowd caused all the noise, shouting and booing, even throwing things.

A hanging was in progress.

She hadn't seen this much activity in Red River Crossing since she'd returned four months ago after graduating from college. Enthused, she decided to join the excitement.

A loud bang, like an explosion, held her in place. What was that?

On the gallows several feet above her, a man staggered

to the edge and tumbled off, landing with a thud almost at her feet.

Adina felt as if her heart had taken the plunge with him. Was he dead? She hurried over and crouched at his side. "Sir?"

No answer. Worried he might have broken a bone, she ran her hands over him, but found nothing.

Her pulse raced as she noticed a pool of blood forming beneath his head. She couldn't see a wound. He wore a cloth hood that covered his entire head. Putting her fingers to the pulse point in his neck, she held her breath, praying to feel a beat.

He was alive! His pulse seemed weak, but he lived.

She closed her eyes, giving thanks.

But it wasn't enough. The poor man's head bled profusely. She had to do something to stop it, or he could die.

Bending over and lifting her skirt, she ripped a strip from her petticoat, then crouched to wrap it around his head, mask and all, tying it in back.

Russell Sandford, the marshal, ran up and knelt on the man's other side. "Kirk? Can you hear me?"

"He's unconscious." Adina made a mental note of the men's names. Having been gone attending college, she only recently returned, and the marshal was new to her.

She doubted the hangman lived in Red River Crossing. "I did what I could to stop the bleeding, but he needs a doctor. Shall I fetch him?"

A deputy hurried over. "What do you want me to do, Marshal?"

Sandford looked up at him. "I sent Henry after the shooter. See if you can calm this crowd and get them to leave. Go up on the gallows so they can see you."

"Will do." The deputy raced off.

Beyond the gallows, people were yelling, asking where the hangman went.

"Tarnation!" Sandford exclaimed. "We've got to get Kirk away from here before those maniacs find him. Grab his feet and help me get him to his wagon."

"Then will we get the doctor?"

"Let's get him settled in his own bed first, shall we? Take his feet."

She did as ordered, though it wasn't easy, with her hands shaking and her heart pounding. The man was big and heavy. They half-carried, half-dragged him into the alley behind the jail where a tinker's cart and mule waited. The thought of what the people searching for him might do if they came upon her and the marshal with a defenseless hangman terrified her, and they could arrive at any moment.

"Set him down while I find his key." The marshal lowered him to the dirt. Gently, she released his feet. Sandford searched Kirk's pockets, came up with a key, lowered the steps from underneath, and opened the door while glancing worriedly at the corner where the mob would appear. Awkwardly, they moved their burden into the wagon. Sandford stepped up first and lugged the man's torso up, and then it was Adina's turn.

"Shut the door when you can," he said.

Still holding the hangman's feet, she climbed a step, lifted, climbed a step, lifted. Once inside, she elbowed the door shut. They had to swing their patient onto the bed at the back, after which Adina collapsed in a huddle on the floor, her long skirts billowing around her.

"Sorry to put you through that." The marshal rested against the wall. "You're strong for a woman. Don't you work for the newspaper?"

"That's right. I'm Adina Kinnaird." She panted a little from her efforts and peered up at him. She considered Russell Sandford one of the best-looking men in Red River Crossing, but as a bachelor, he had plenty of women competing for his attention. "I only work part-time, though.

I'm a writer. You must have moved here while I was at college."

"The mayor's my uncle and got me the job here. I guess it's been six months now." He straightened and bent to look at Kirk's face. "He's still out. I need to get back and make sure my deputies control that crowd. I hope it's a long time before we have another hanging. Can you watch him until I get back? I'm worried that blow to his head could have caused a concussion. It might not be good for him to sleep very long."

She moved to sit on the edge of the bed, placing her fingers on Kirk's wrist to check his pulse. "I have nowhere to go other than home, and I can skip supper if necessary. I have an apple in my bag. His heartbeat's regular. That's a good sign. You could bring the doctor here if you're concerned. I think it would be a good idea."

The marshal shook his head. "Kirk wouldn't like that. He doesn't want anyone to know where to find him or what he looks like. I'm afraid this job has made him distrustful of people. It's a shame because he was a fine minister before this, in Nampa, where I grew up."

"I wondered because of the way he talked to the prisoner when the man was terrified. Kirk was so compassionate and kind; he sounded like a minister."

"That's him for you. I've known him for years."

"Why was everyone so cruel to him?" Adina frowned. "I guess I can understand that man shooting at him because he'd killed his friend or whatever, but the way the townsfolk acted shocked me. They have no reason to hate Kirk. People I've met who seemed perfectly normal, sane, and kind were throwing rotten food at him."

"It isn't him," Stanford said. "It's his job. Folks hate hangmen for some reason. I don't understand it. Someone has to do it. Like you said, it's one thing if they cared about the prisoner, but these people didn't know him, and the man Dunstan killed was a stranger on a stagecoach he'd held up, so no one knew him either. People are strange."

"Well..." She placed her hand over Kirk's where it lay on the bed. "I have nothing against him."

"Good. I'll leave him in your care and check on my deputies. Don't worry. I won't abandon you. I'll return as soon as I can." He pushed away from the wall.

"All right. I hope everything is okay."

"Me too." He handed her the key. "Lock up after me." He went out, and she secured the door.

Alone, Adina studied the man on the bed, wishing she could see his face. Not out of curiosity—although there was that—but mostly to make sure the bleeding had stopped and see what kind of wound the bullet had left him with. He might need stitches, and she still thought a doctor should see him.

He moaned and moved slightly as if uncomfortable. The bed wasn't long enough for such a tall man. His head nearly touched one end, and his feet angled toward the edge of the mattress because there wasn't enough room. Having his boots off would help, and that was something she could do. She began tugging on one. A moan took her gaze to Kirk's head, wishing she could see his face. He rolled his head to the side as if to keep the injury from touching the bed. Was he coming to?

When he stopped moving and seemed *out* again, she removed the boot and went to work on the other one. After setting them on the floor, she wondered if he might be cold and glanced around for a blanket. She had just found one in a cubbyhole under the bed when someone knocked on the door.

"It's Russell," the visitor called.

She unlocked the door, and he motioned for her to come outside.

Adina took the time to throw the blanket over Kirk before obeying. "Hello, Marshal."

"Call me Russell," Russell said when she joined him.

"Could you drive this rig?"

She stepped to the side and glanced at the mule hitched to the wagon. It didn't take much to guess what the marshal had in mind. "I'd be a little nervous trying to handle the mule. I understand they can be temperamental. But I used to drive my aunt's buggy to take her shopping."

"Good. I can't guarantee there won't be problems, but those blasted people are still looking for Kirk. Some strangers are keeping the crowd worked up. I'm sure it's on purpose, and I plan to find out by arresting them, but first, I want Kirk away from here and safe. Will you drive him up the river road, and I'll come and get you later?"

"I'll do my best, Marshal." What else could she say? She couldn't very well lie and say she couldn't do it. She didn't want him to think badly of her, and she did want to help. There had been nothing for her to do at the newspaper office, so, hopefully, her boss wouldn't miss her.

"Great. But I told you to call me Russell."

"Okay, Russell."

"That's the way." He gave her arm a gentle squeeze. "I knew I could count on you. Once you reach the end of the road, there's a narrow lane—a trail, honestly—but you can drive on it. Cottonwood trees line the way. About a mile up, you'll find a spot big enough to park the wagon close to the trees, and there's an old campfire near the water. I like to fish there when I get the chance. Don't go on the other side of the path. That's private property, so keep to the riverside."

"Okay, but then what?" She climbed up to the driver's seat, willing but not thrilled with this assignment. She felt sorry for Kirk and wanted to help him; if only she didn't have to deal with a mule. They frightened her, which was silly because she loved horses. The last thing she wanted was to be a prissy female who couldn't handle a wagon and mule in front of Russell. "I truly feel he needs medical attention. Maybe stitches."

Marshal Sandford nodded, his eyes filled with concern and apprehension. He no doubt felt torn between his friendship with Kirk and his duties. "I'll bring first-aid supplies when I return," he said. "That's the best I can do. If folks see me visiting the doctor, they'll wonder why and if it has to do with Kirk. I can't risk the wrong person following me out here. Someone wants him dead."

"Oh, my heavens." Appalled, Adina adjusted her place on the hard wooden seat and took the reins. Her heart raced, driven by fresh fear for Kirk and a growing need to get away from town. "I'd better leave."

"Yes, please. Once you get the wagon parked, put some

rocks under the wheels so they won't roll, and remember to set the brake."

"I will." She flicked the reins and clucked to the mule. He didn't move.

The marshal walked over and swatted the ornery critter on the rump, and he took off.

"Thanks." She waved to him as the mule plodded up the dirt lane. With trepidation, she glanced down each alley she came to, worried she'd run into someone who'd try to stop her, but saw only a few children playing ball.

The river road was rough and narrow enough in many places that the wheels rode on grass on each side. She drove slowly, careful not to hit any holes and jostle Kirk. She wondered about his last name and how he would react when he came to and saw her. He didn't know her, after all.

What kind of man would take a job hanging men? Was he sadistic? He hadn't seemed that way when he talked to the prisoner. He'd been kind and reassuring. Maybe he did this work out of kindness, to help the men condemned to hang. The more she thought about it, the more curious she became. The writer inside her ached to know his background and how he thought.

Various scenarios popped into her head. Someone

special to him had been hanged, and, worried about how frightened the person had been, he wanted to help others in the same situation. Or he'd almost been hanged himself, and the terror made him want to ease the way for people faced with a similar fate. If he were older, he might have lost a son to a wrongful hanging. Maybe he'd simply seen a hanging and felt sorry for the victim. Whatever his reasons, she found it impossible to believe they weren't altruistic.

As she drove, she enjoyed watching the river swirl and gurgle as if they were in a race. She might have laughed at her chances of winning against such an opponent if she hadn't been on such a serious mission. As Russell Sandford had said, tree after tree lined the way until she finally reached a spot big enough for the wagon. She smiled to see a fire pit near the river. Driving as close to the trees as she dared, she stopped, set the brake, and jumped down.

The mule brayed, wanting to go to the river. "Just a second," she said, impatient to check on Kirk. After staking the animal where he could reach water and grass, she unlocked the door and went inside. Kirk remained lying on his back, eyes closed. Relieved that he seemed no worse, she sat on the edge of the mattress and leaned over to see if his head still bled. At finding it dry, she said a silent prayer of thanks.

Wanting to check his wound more thoroughly and clean him up, she reached for the bottom button on the hood's side, then stopped. Russell had said Kirk didn't want people to see him. After what happened in town, she could understand but wouldn't hold off forever. That hood and the blood she believed had likely crept underneath enhanced his chances of the wound becoming infected, which she refused to risk happening.

Kirk opened his eyes with trepidation, unsure whether to expect to see angels flying about fluffy clouds strumming stringed instruments or the devil stirring a bloody cauldron over a blazing fire.

Why would he even think such a thing?

Oh, yes, the hanging. He'd been shot and assumed he was dying. To see that he was in his wagon left him uncertain whether to be glad or disappointed. *Don't be ridiculous, man.* He still lived, which had to be better than the alternative. But how had he gotten here?

Russell must have brought him. At least that mob of crazy people hadn't gotten hold of him. He shuddered inside to think what might have happened to him then.

A movement took his gaze to the door where a young woman stood looking outside, the door ajar. Who was she, and how had she gotten in his wagon?

"Wha-what are you doing in here?" he asked.

The woman spun toward him. "Oh, good. You're awake." She shut the door and hurried to the bed.

Kirk stared at her until the pain in his head derailed his attention. She was so pretty, it had him thinking of angels again, except her hair was dark, and he'd thought angels would be blonde. He moved slightly, thinking to sit up, and pain stabbed through his head. He moaned, reached up, and felt the bandage. "Am I badly hurt?"

"Yes, you were shot," she said.

He remembered the hanging, pulling the lever, and Dunstan falling. Then some man galloped up, yelling, *Stop!* Right after that, he'd felt a sharp pain, and everything became fuzzy, but he figured he'd been shot. He'd heard a gun go off.

"The bullet left a groove in the side of your head," the woman said.

It surprised him that he liked her being there even

though she was a stranger. He wasn't alone. Kirk spent nearly all his time alone—one of the main drawbacks of this job, though the number one reason was what the position required him to do. Blast it, he was a preacher, not a killer. Taking a life was a sin. He would go to hell now.

For the sake of his beloved brother, Cage.

That was what he kept telling himself whenever he considered ending it: he had to hang people to save his little brother. What a rotten way to live.

"I'm Adina Kinnaird," the woman said. "I saw you fall from the gallows and was trying to help you when the marshal came, and we brought you here. He had me drive your wagon out of town to avoid the insane people looking for you. I was terrified they'd hurt you even worse. The damage to your head is bad enough, but you'll also have bruises from the fall. Luckily, you didn't break anything."

Yes, the fall. He remembered the severe pain in his head, followed by a falling sensation. After that, everything went blank. "I'm Kirk Reddick. Did Russell catch the man who shot me?"

"I don't know." The woman, Adina frowned, perhaps surprised he remembered anything. "The marshal will be here later. He stayed behind to control the crowd and find the man who hurt you."

He felt his head again, relieved that he still wore the hood. He glanced at her. "Did you bandage me?"

"Yes, but it's imperative I remove that mask and clean your wound. We can't risk infection. The marshal said he'd bring some medicine."

"You can't take off my hood. I don't want you to see my face."

She smiled gently. "Kirk, I don't care about who you are or what you do for a living. I'm not about to share anything I learn about you with anyone else."

"You aren't a reporter, are you?"

"No. I work for the newspaper but only as a typist. I promise I have no intention of telling my employer about you. He'd want to interview you and write a story for the paper. I wouldn't do that to you. I just want to help."

"Why?"

She stared at him, taken aback by the question. "That's what you do for people. Haven't you ever helped anyone for no reason except it's the right thing to do?"

As a minister, he had helped many people, and she was right; it was the right thing—the Christian thing. "I'm sorry. It's been so long since anyone except Russell has been kind to me."

She frowned, her eyes and mouth reflecting sympathy.

"It's a sin how people treat you."

Abruptly, she changed moods, smiling and causing him to blink in surprise.

"Listen, can I get you anything?" she asked. "Some water, maybe?"

"Yes, I could use a drink."

He struggled to sit up, and she rushed to help him, stuffing pillows behind his back.

"There, I'll get your water now, except I don't see how you'll drink it if you refuse to take off that hood."

"Oh, you're right." But he didn't dare remove it. Could he trust her? She had been unusually caring so far, but it was his safety they were talking about, and she worked for a newspaper.

She eyed him speculatively as she waited. Then she lifted a chain over her head and held it out. An engraved, heart-shaped locket swung from the gold links. "This locket holds the only photos I have of my parents. They died when I was six, and an aunt who lives here in Red River Crossing raised me. I've been away at college and just returned a few months ago. Jason at the newspaper was desperate enough for help to take a chance on me, not as a reporter but as a simple typist. You can keep this for as long as we're together if you'll just trust me enough to let me make sure you aren't getting infection under that hood."

He stared at the locket, and she opened it to show him her parents' photos. A handsome couple stared back at him, almost as if begging him to give in.

"You said you'd been at college." He saw intelligence in her eyes. "Did you finish? What was your goal?"

"I have an English degree now." Her grin and a charming dimple to the right of her mouth showed her pride in being able to say that. "I hope to become a writer. Not a reporter. I want to be a novelist. I've written a few stories but have always been rejected. They don't publish women. Because their books don't sell, they said. I wanted to say, what about Charlotte Bronte, Jane Austen, Louisa May Alcott, Emily Dickinson, and others? But I didn't have the nerve."

She had a point there. It wasn't right for them to refuse to publish women because of their gender. It had often troubled him how everyone seemed to place males above females. His mother had been brilliant. She was the one who truly ran the family transport business. Whenever his father needed to know what wagons were available, who was making what delivery, or what orders were being handled, he had to ask Mother. Kirk had greatly admired and respected her.

Women still couldn't vote. Some states continued to deny them the right to own property. However, that had nothing to do with the matter at hand: whether he could trust her to keep quiet about his identity and location.

"If you want proof," she continued, "I'd be glad to let you read something of mine. I love words, the meanings, the connotations. I want to spend my life working with words."

"I can see how your face lights up just talking about it. I think you're serious, and I've always believed if you want something badly enough, you'll get it somehow. God listens to our prayers and knows what's in our hearts. I think you'll attain your goal." He held out the necklace. "I don't need to hold onto this. You may remove my hood. I know you'll be careful."

"Yes, I will. Thank you for trusting me. I trust you, too. I know you won't take advantage of me being alone in here with you. I heard what you said to the prisoner when he lost courage and found it inspiring. He was visibly touched, as I was."

"Why, thank you, Miss Kinnaird." He smiled, appreciating her praise. He'd never intended for anyone other than the prisoner to hear those words. Even so, it was nice to know someone thought well of them.

She replaced the necklace around her neck, tucking it inside her bodice. "I'll need some water. Alcohol would be better."

"You can use my name, Kirk. I keep a bottle of whiskey for that very purpose in the cupboard directly left of the bed."

"Call me Adina." She found it and poured some into a bowl from another cupboard. It had been opened, but if anyone used it, they hadn't taken much. "Now for that hood," she said, sitting beside him on the edge of the bed. "I'll be very gentle."

He nodded. Why was this lovely young woman still single? Were the men of Red River Crossing blind? Was his friend, Russell, blind? Why hadn't he snatched her up? She was a pleasure to look at, intelligent and efficient. He knew the effort it took to drive this wagon, yet she'd done it to save his life. In his book, that made her a heroine.

With great care, she unwrapped the bandage she'd applied earlier. "The wound has stopped bleeding. That's good. I'll be able to judge it more fully after getting the hood off." Slowly and carefully, she unbuttoned the left side of the hood, then lifted the edges. Gently, she inched the fabric over his mouth, nose, and eyes.

"Now, the tricky part," she said, biting her lower lip. "I can't disturb the wound, or it might start bleeding again."

While she worked on him—her face near enough for him to see every detail—he admired her well-defined mouth, pert nose, and eyes the blue of the forget-me-nots in mountain meadows. Long curving lashes shaded them, and above, her brows arched perfectly to do their part, adding to her natural beauty.

He nearly chuckled as he scolded himself for paying so much attention to the girl's appearance. It wasn't as if he could court her, even if he wanted to. Kirk was in no position to offer a woman a home, marriage, children, or a future. He didn't know what his own future held.

Millimeter by millimeter, Adina lifted the fabric of the hood until, at last, it came free, and she dropped it to the floor. Letting out a long breath, she said, "There we go. Oh, you have lovely thick hair. I love the color. It makes me think of chocolate, and it's just dark enough to make your minty green eyes stand out like beacons."

He chuckled at her description. He never would have called his eyes minty. She made him sound handsome. Was that how she saw him?

She leaned back to peer at him. "I can see your wound clearly now. It's deeper than I'd hoped and will likely leave a scar. You might need to grow your hair longer to cover it, but it won't mar your looks."

"I guess I can live with that." Her comment about his appearance made him want to ask if she found him handsome. The sound of hoofbeats nearing the wagon saved him from his foolishness.

Chapter Three

Wishing she had a rifle or six-gun, Adina excused herself to go outside and peer around the corner of the wagon to see who was approaching. Hopefully, they'd just ride on past.

The rider waved, and she recognized the marshal.

She stepped out into the open as he reined in. "I'm glad to see you, Marshal."

"Thought I told you to call me Russell." He swung down from the saddle. "Is everything all right? Did Kirk wake up?"

"Yes, *Russell*, and I got him to let me remove his hood and clean him up a little, but he doesn't want a doctor to see him, and I think he needs stitches."

"I'm impressed that you handled him so well. He can be stubborn. I'll look at him." He opened the door. "It's Russ, Kirk. I've come to check on you."

Adina followed him inside. He set a flour bag on the tiny counter.

Kirk rolled over and sat up. "Hello, Russ."

"How are you feeling?" Russell sat beside him. "Adina says you need stitches. I can do them if you want. I'm experienced."

Kirk turned a little so the marshal could examine his wound better. "I'd trust you more than a doctor. I know you'll keep quiet about where I am."

"So would Doc Ames, Kirk. You can trust him, but if you want, I'll take care of these now before more time passes. We don't want the skin to dry out too much before we get it done. That bullet left quite a gully in your head. Lucky it didn't go deeper, or your brains would've spilled out."

Kirk chuckled. "Wouldn't that have been a fine mess?"

"Indeed." Russell stood. "I'm going to get a few things from my saddlebag. Be right back."

Kirk looked up at Adina, who was frowning. "You don't appreciate dark humor, eh?"

"If you're referring to you two joking about your brains

falling out, I get it. It just didn't make me laugh. But I do enjoy hearing you laugh." She smiled. "It sounds a little rusty, as if you don't do it often enough."

"Sorry. I'll try to be more jovial."

She rolled her eyes. "Just be natural and relax."

He grinned. "You amuse me. That should help."

Kirk's looks put Russell's to shame, especially when he smiled as he did now. If not for his job, he should be able to find a wife easily. She might consider applying for the position if it existed.

Russell returned, laid out his supplies on the bed, took hold of Kirk's jaw, and moved the man's head so he could see the wound well in the light from the window over the bed. Adina stood nearby to help.

First, the marshal handed Kirk a stick. "Bite on this if it hurts too much."

Kirk put it in his mouth. Adina handed the marshal a cloth soaked in alcohol to sterilize the wound. Finished, he laid it down. "Give me the needle there threaded with fishing line."

"Fishing line?" she said. "You had nothing better?"

"Nope, and it works well for this."

She gave it to him, and he began closing Kirk's wound.

Adina watched in amazement. He did an excellent job, using tiny stitches that would barely leave a scar.

When he finished, he stepped back and wiped moisture from his forehead.

"Beautiful work, Marshal," Adina told him. "I mean Russell. A doctor couldn't have done better."

"Thanks, Adina. How about you bandage it? You did a exemplary job before, and I need a break."

"All right." She turned away, bent and tore another strip from her petticoat, then traded places with Russell and set to work. Finished, she asked, "Is there anything more I can do for you, Kirk?"

He took the stick from his mouth and handed it to her. It had no teeth marks she could see, which meant he was a very brave man. Maybe the stitches hadn't hurt too badly. She gave it to Russell, who threw it outside.

"I need to get back to town," Russell said. "You did a fine job of parking this rig, Adina. Kirk, will you be okay here by yourself? There's a fire pit outside, and I noticed Adina or someone piled some wood by it."

"I'll be fine," Kirk replied, lying down again. "I think I'll mostly be sleeping."

"Don't forget to eat," Adina told him. "You need your strength."

Russell pointed to the flour sack on the counter. "I brought you some supplies: cans of beans and fruit, some jerky, and biscuits from the bakery. They'll be cold now but still tasty."

"That sounds good. I do have some canned goods and water in containers. I'll be fine. Take Adina back. I don't want her losing her job on my account."

"Are you sure? You won't need me to help?" she asked, uncertain about leaving him alone. Part of her just plain didn't want to go. She wasn't ready to examine that too closely.

"Yes. Thank you for caring and helping me. I won't forget it. And I'll be fine here. If anyone comes, I'll say I'm a traveling preacher. It's worked before."

"And it's true, in a way. You are technically a preacher, and you're traveling." Russell offered his hand, and they shook. "We'll leave then. Ready, Adina?"

She shrugged. "I guess so. I had nothing with me, so I don't have to worry about leaving anything behind."

"Let's go then." He opened the door, stepped down, and offered her a hand.

She didn't need assistance but laid her palm against his and descended.

"Bye, Kirk," he called inside. "I'll be by tomorrow to

check on you."

"Yes," Adina added with little enthusiasm. Her chest felt tight, her eyes moist. "Goodbye. It was nice meeting you."

A faint farewell came from Kirk, and Russell shut the door. "We have to ride double," he said, leading Adina to his buckskin gelding. "Climb on."

She hefted herself into the saddle, removed her foot from the stirrup, adjusted her skirts, and scooted forward as far as possible to give him room to sit. He swung up behind her, took the reins, and the horse started forward.

Adina looked back at the wagon, worried about Kirk and hating to leave him alone. She hoped he got up and locked the door. And that no one found him.

The first thing Adina noticed as she walked to work the following day was that the gallows had been dismantled and hauled away. After the arduous day she'd had yesterday following the hanging, she'd gone straight to bed the previous night when Russell dropped her off at her home. She hadn't seen or talked to anyone.

Three times, dreams of Kirk being in danger had awakened her. In the last one, a man with a gun threatened them both. Kirk had saved her and then kissed her. Smiling, she put her fingers to her lips as if she could still feel his mouth against hers. The poor man must always be in peril because of his work. It wasn't fair.

The second thing she noticed was the exasperated expression on her boss's face when she entered the newspaper office. Jason Johanson wasn't a remarkably handsome man, and when he frowned as he did now, he could almost be frightening. His black hair, worn long, his hawk nose and prominent cheekbones, gave him the look of a fierce Indian, and his expression right now could make a person anticipate being scalped. All he needed was a tomahawk to make the image complete.

"And just where were you all day yesterday?" he asked when she walked to her desk and put her bag in a drawer.

She hesitated, debating what to say. She couldn't mention Kirk. "I was helping a sick man with Marshal Sandford."

"Oh, never mind that I needed help with the paper," Jason replied sarcastically.

"I'm sorry," Adina said.

Was Kirk all right this morning? She wished she could visit him. She didn't know him well, yet she felt a strong attraction to him. "It was an emergency. I had no choice. How could I tell the marshal no? I'll try to make it up to you. I can work late, maybe?"

He went to the press and fiddled with one of the knobs holding the ink rollers in place. He calmed down, and his tone became conciliatory. "I had trouble with the press that there was nothing you could have done anything about. I may have to send for new rollers. You know how hard they are to hang onto when you're loading them. I dropped one."

"Oh no!" Adina exclaimed. "Is it ruined?"

"Yeah. It has a big dent and won't spread the ink evenly."

"I'm sorry, Mr. Johanson. If I'd been here, I could have helped hold it. No wonder you're angry with me." She didn't know him well, having worked there only three months, but she still didn't like disappointing him. Hopefully, he wouldn't let her go.

"No." He waved a hand at her. "I'm strong enough. I should have been able to hang onto it. At least it happened after I finished printing the papers."

"Did you get them distributed? I could do that for you

while you work on the press."

After tinkering a moment more, he looked at her. "Yes. That would be helpful. They're stacked over there by the door."

She looked over and saw them stuffed in the unique bag made for carrying them. She took one out to read it and found what she'd expected—the hanging plastered all over the front page as if something to be excited about. She'd hoped he'd not make so much out of the shooting and other violence perpetrated by the townspeople. They'd broken a window, shot holes into store walls, and tipped over benches. "I'll start delivering these right now."

Jason left the press and came over to her. "Let me help you get the bag on."

He held up the double-sided bag, slipping the straps over her shoulders, fastening them so that a pouch rested against each hip. Then he opened the door for her. He didn't bother to say thanks, but he never did. From what she'd overheard at the café once, he'd been married and had a small son, but his wife got tired of his sullen attitude and moved to Boise, taking the boy with her. Adina suspected he missed them.

The first place she went was the jail. Marshal Sandford

sat at his desk. "I brought this week's paper for you, Marshal. How many do you want?

"Here, I'll take three." He stood and held out his hand. "I always read it, and then I'll see if my prisoner wants one. I have to make sure there isn't anything in there I don't want him to know, like what evidence the court will have against him."

"Oh!" She glanced toward the door to the cells and leaned closer to whisper, "The man who shot Kirk?"

"That's the one."

"Did he say why he did it?"

"Didn't need to. It was obvious. Kirk had just hung his partner. But I asked anyway, and my theory was correct."

Adina shuddered, remembering the hanging and Kirk falling from the gallows. The handsome hangman hadn't been far from her thoughts since. "Jason wrote about it in the paper."

"Thanks." He took them and sat.

"Did you check on Kirk today?" she asked as he opened the two-page newspaper.

"I rode out early. He was up and about. You better go if you want to see him again, or he'll be gone. He has another hanging tomorrow in De Lamar."

Adina frowned. She wanted to see him again, but how

would she get out there? "Do you know if Mr. Hobbs still rents out horses at the livery?"

"You need a way to reach Kirk?"

"Yes."

"How about I rent a buggy and take you?" he said. "I need to see him before he leaves."

Her eyes flashed pleasure. "Oh, that would be great. I'll have to see if my boss will let me off. He's not happy with me missing work yesterday."

"We could leave as soon as you get off work today. You wouldn't have to miss any time that way, and Kirk won't be leaving until tomorrow morning."

"Wonderful." Impulsively, she kissed him on the cheek.

"Hey." He smiled. "You keep doing that, and I'll have to start courting you."

"You're a tease, you know that?" she accused. "I'd better deliver the rest of the papers."

"See you later then."

Relieved to have worked out a plan to see Kirk again, Adina left the jail with a lightness to her step that hadn't been there before. Russell Sandford, a nice man. At twenty-two, he was four years older than Adina. She wasn't sure she'd mind if he did court her. He'd make a good husband and likely a good father. But she was getting ahead of herself. She didn't even know if he genuinely liked her. And there was Kirk. She was very attracted to him. Despite what he did for a living, he was a good man and so pleasant to look at. She wondered what her parents would say to her marrying a hangman. They weren't the type to be prejudiced, but she remembered what Russell said about the families of hangmen being mistreated. Her parents would worry about her. She supposed she should, too. Besides, she had no idea when he'd be in Red River Crossing again. Not until another killer needed hanging, and that wasn't something she could look forward to. Truthfully, it was silly to even think of a future with a man nearly gone from her life and unlikely to return.

After leaving the rest of the papers off at the stores and hotels that kept them handy for customers, she returned to the newspaper office. A beautiful horse stood out front. Someone to see Jason? The black gelding turned his head to look at her as she walked by. He had a white face with a black mark in the center, forming a perfect cross. A bright red saddle blanket contrasted sharply with his dark coloring. She suspected whoever owned him liked things that were showy. Entering through the front, she looked for Jason. Not seeing him, she called up the stairs beside the door, "Jason, I'm back."

He didn't answer. Must be busy. He had to be in his apartment upstairs, though. If he'd left, he would have locked the door. She went to her desk to see if he'd left any notes or work to do. Two handwritten letters lay there, one to the printing press company and another to the paper supply store. She removed the cover from her typewriter and sat down to type up the letters.

After three sentences, a loud thud on the ceiling had her glancing up and wondering what Jason did to cause such a noise. With a sigh, she continued typing, finished the first letter, and started on the second.

More thumps came from upstairs, along with some yelling. Worried her boss might be in trouble, Adina rose and went to the stairs. She'd opened her mouth to call up to Jason when she heard a strange voice say, "Drat you, Jason. I trusted you."

"My paper is floundering," Jason retorted. "I can't afford to pass up a juicy story about a man framing another for bank robbery right here in our county."

"I told you that in confidence," his visitor claimed, "not to save your blasted paper."

A whacking sound came that Adina could have sworn sounded like one man hitting another. A loud curse followed, and then a sharp *bang*.

A shot!

Good heavens! Adina jumped back.

Had Jason's visitor shot him? Or was it the other way around? What should she do?

Get the marshal! a voice in her head cried.

Not wasting a moment, she ran to get her bag and then back to the door, terrified the shooter might come down and shoot her before she could escape. As she turned the doorknob, she glanced up the stairs and saw the killer looking straight down at her. His eyes seemed to glow in the dim shadows of the stairwell. He paused, reaching for a six-gun in a holster on his hip.

Gulping, Adina didn't wait one more second. She yanked open the door, expecting to feel a bullet drill into her back any second. Her heart pounded furiously as she darted outside. On impulse, she decided to lock the door. He could shoot at her through the glass but couldn't come after her.

Her pulse soared when she saw he'd almost reached the bottom of the stairs. Her hands shook so badly she dropped the keys.

No! Calm down, Adina. The killer's almost here!

At last, she thrust the key into the lock, and the bolt slid home. The man who'd shot Jason was trapped in the office now. Through the window, he glared at her with pale blue eyes. He had wild, blond, curly hair and a grim, frowning mouth. The horse beside her—his horse?—whinnied nervously and stamped his hooves, startling her and jolting her into action.

She loosened the reins from the hitching post and slapped the horse on the rump, sending it racing down the street, certain it must belong to the murderer. A pounding behind her had her looking over her shoulder at the office door, where the killer was mouthing curses at her and jiggling the knob. Adina picked up her skirts and ran.

A minute later, she threw open the jail door and shouted the marshal's name. He looked up from the stove where he'd been pouring coffee. The hot liquid sloshed over his hand, and he cursed. "Confound it, Adina. You made me scald my hand."

"Sorry!" She bounced on her heels impatiently. "But Jason might be dead or hurt. I heard arguing upstairs, then a shot and a man came running down. You need to hurry to the newspaper office." She grabbed for his hand.

"Sakes alive." He jerked away. "Take a deep breath,

calm yourself, and tell me what happened."

She felt slightly faint and shivered as a cold chill shot down her spine. "I told you, I heard loud thumps and shouting in Jason's upstairs apartment. He was arguing with a man. Then I heard a gunshot. When I reached the door to leave, a man was coming down. I locked the office so he can't get out."

"Adina, did he see you?"

"Yes."

"Stay here. You're in grave danger. Give me the key so I can get inside."

She pulled the key from her skirt pocket and handed it to him.

"Whatever you do, don't come to the newspaper office, all right?" He strode to the door.

"Good luck. Don't get shot." Sudden fear for him shot her pulse back up from where she'd begun to calm down as she watched him run toward the newspaper office next door. Inside her head, a plea repeated itself: *Please be all right, Jason. Please don't get shot, Russell.*

Despite his orders, she couldn't sit there while her friend placed himself in danger. She had to at least watch from outside. Maybe she could find one of the deputies if she saw he was in trouble. Where were they all anyway?

Shouldn't they be here?

The marshal was unlocking the door when she stepped onto the boardwalk.

No! she wanted to yell. The killer was still inside. She had to keep Russell from being shot.

A weapon, that's what she needed. Darting back inside, she found a gun rack and a six-shooter sitting there. Grabbing it, she raced out the door. Her heart threatened to bolt right out of her chest when she saw the newspaper office door open and no one in sight. Marshal Sandford must be inside. He might even now be fighting with the killer. She plastered herself to the wall beside the door and peered inside.

All was silent.

Had the killer escaped? She searched the street. Shops were closing up as it was nearly suppertime. People crowded the boardwalks. She saw no black horse and no man with light, curly hair.

Deciding she had to make sure Marshal Sandford was all right, she started up the stairs, her heart trying to jump out of her chest. Terrified what she might see as she reached the top, she held up the six-gun with both hands and peeked into the apartment. Jason lay on the floor in a pool of blood. The marshal knelt beside him.

"Oh, no." She lowered the gun and raced over to them. "Is he dead?"

"What are you doing here?" Sandford got to his feet. "Didn't I tell you to stay put?"

"I couldn't just sit there, not knowing what was happening. I wanted to help."

He snatched the gun from her and stuck it in his back waistband. "Did you see anyone before you came up here?"

"No, the office looked empty."

"There were signs that someone did some searching. Looking for you, I think. Do you have somewhere you can go for a few days? Maybe stay with a relative or friend? I want you to stay away from the office and your house."

"No. Russell, I'm alone in the world. I have nowhere to go. My aunt is dead. She left me the house. I don't even have a friend here. I've only been back in Red River a few months since I graduated college."

He paced the plank floor with consternation. At last, he stopped. "All right. I have an idea. I'll take you home so you can pack a bag. Then I'm taking you to Kirk."

"Kirk!" Her brow furrowed. "Where would I sleep? There's only one bed, and he's injured. I can't put him out of his bed."

Rubbing his forehead, he frowned. "I know. I have a

tent you can use. Come with me while I get it."

"Okay."

He locked up the office, grabbed her hand, and dragged her to the jail. "Wait here." He went down the hall, opened a door, and disappeared for several minutes. When he returned, he carried a canvas bag and a bulging flour sack. "Let's go."

She followed him out, waited while he attached the bag to his saddle and shoved the sack into his saddlebags.

"I got a tip," he said while he worked, "about one of the bank robbers from the gang Dunstan ran, riding a black horse and sent my deputy looking for it."

"A black horse? With a red saddle blanket?" she asked, remembering the horse at the office.

"I don't know about the blanket. Why?"

He lifted her into the saddle and swung on behind her.

"There was a black horse at the hitching post outside the office when I went to work this morning. He had a white face, with a black cross, and a red saddle blanket. I thought it might be the killer's, so I shooed it away before I came to you."

"Confound it." He looked around nervously. "Who knows where the shooter is now?"

At her house, he lifted her down and waited in the parlor while she stuffed a few necessities into a small valise.

"I'm ready." She had changed into a split skirt, shirt, and a warm coat.

He said nothing, just led her back outside, waited while she mounted his horse, jumped behind, and nudged the mare into a trot. Once they'd left the town behind, he urged the gelding to a gallop.

Please still be there, Kirk. And take me with you willingly.

Fear had her sweating beneath her cotton bodice. She felt the moisture dribble between her breasts and under her arms. She should remove her coat but would likely fall off the horse.

Russell changed direction toward the river, and she recognized the trail she'd used before. They reached the spot where he'd been camped, and her heart sank.

"He's gone. What do we do now?" she asked.

"He can't have gone far." Russell clucked his tongue and got the horse moving again. "Let's see if we can catch up to him."

They traveled what seemed like miles to Adina, with her nerves on edge. Then there he was, just ahead, his wagon lumbering along at the speed of a turtle.

Russell quickly caught up and stopped Kirk. "Got a

problem I'm hoping you can fix for our friend Adina here."

"I'd be glad to help." Kirk climbed down from the seat. He still wore the bandage they'd put on him but looked stronger. "What do I need to do?"

Russell dismounted and lifted Adina down. "This morning, someone shot and killed her boss at the newspaper office. The killer knows Adina saw him."

"No! I'm sorry, Adina. Are you out of a job now?"

"I assume so."

Russell spoke up. "I'm worried whoever killed Jason will want to silence Adina, so I brought her to you, hoping you'd take her along."

A satirical half-smile formed on Kirk's face. "And you think she'd be safe with me? I'm a hangman, remember? A lot of people would like to see me dead."

"I know, but I couldn't think of a safer place to take her." Russell put his hands on his hips and paced the grassy spot where they'd stopped. "At least you know how to use a gun, and the killer won't be looking for a couple. That might help where you're concerned, too. Folks see a woman with you, and they won't think you're the hangman."

Kirk looked thoughtful. "You might have a point there, and Lord knows I need all the protection I can get, but where would she sleep? I don't—"

"I have that covered," Russell interrupted. "I brought a tent and also some food supplies. She knows how to start a fire and cook over the flames. Right, Adina?"

"Yes, my family used to go camping so Pa could hunt." It just hit her that she could write Kirk's story, and maybe it would help all hangmen if people understood why they took that line of work. But she'd need to introduce that idea at the right moment. Kirk wasn't likely to take to it right away. She did have another idea, though. "I thought maybe I could help you prove your brother's innocence."

"I sure would like to find the robber who framed him. More than you could imagine."

"If you find him," Russell said, "you bring him to me. I'll take care of the rest. We'll get you and Cage out from under this lousy sentence the judge gave."

Kirk gave an uncertain shake of his head. "That would be a dream come true for Cage."

"And for you," Adina added.

"I'm more concerned for my brother."

The marshal mounted his horse. Before riding away, he said, "Watch for that horse, Adina. If you see it, wire me."

"A horse?" Kirk asked.

She waved at Russell. "Yes, I'll tell you about it once we're on our way."

Chapter Four

Berle had beaten the backbone into her. His cruelty and unfairness made her want to fight him, particularly when he went after her children. Still, Kirk had gotten his share, and because he loved his little brother, he'd taken Cage's portion. Kirk had doubts now about it being the right thing to do. Maybe Cage would have more inner strength now if he'd suffered his own punishments. The boy was a good man but liked gambling and was weak-willed. In rare moments, Kirk wondered if Cage had lied about being framed for that bank robbery. If Kirk learned it was true, he'd be tempted to thoroughly pound his brother

Cage had no idea of how big a sacrifice Kirk had made

so he could be free, and it was more than sending him to college. This job he'd taken in his brother's place was far worse than he'd anticipated. Even if someone had warned him of how people would look at him and treat him, he wouldn't have believed it then.

He did now.

To think he had been a well-liked and respected minister with a church of his own and a large, loyal congregation who treated him like a prince, to come down to this degrading position in society where he was hated and ridiculed. It wore on his heart like a steel rasp. He hated it with a passion he would only have ever expected to feel for a woman he loved, something he'd never have now. What woman could love a man at the bottom of the social ladder, a man she would be placing herself in harm's way to love?

Kirk glanced sideways at Adina. She was brave to be seen with him. He really should let her know what she was getting herself into. How had she landed a job with a newspaper office, usually reserved for men? Had she gone to a special school or gotten an extraordinary degree or awards?

"Tell me about yourself," he said as they followed the road through a meadow bright with sunflowers and sunshine.

You know about my parents. My Aunt Rose raised me from the time I was six until I went off to college. She passed away my second year in school and left me her house in Red River Crossing where I live now.

Kirk smiled. "First, please call me Kirk, Miss Kinnaird. We're going to be traveling together. No need to keep up the formalities."

She chuckled. "Don't be a hypocrite, Kirk. If I'm to use your given name, you should use mine."

"All I have is my brother."

"You feel responsible for him, don't you?" she asked. "How old is he?"

This woman seemed too sharp for him to sidestep her questions or lie to her. "He's eighteen and I confess, I do feel a need to watch out for him. Our father would have killed him, beating him the way he did us all. Cage was always on the weak side, unhealthy, you know?"

"I understand." She laid a comforting hand on his arm. "Where is he now?"

"In St. Louis, studying the law." He wanted to put his hand over hers; it felt so good to be touched like that, with kindness and empathy—someone rare for him to receive—but she removed it.

"And I bet you're paying for his education." She

paused and looked at him in that way of hers, making him feel like she was peeking inside his head, yet he could see she approved of his efforts to help Cage. "Does your brother have anything to do with you being a hangman instead of a preacher?"

He glanced away. "I don't talk about that. Would you like to stop for something to eat? We'll be reaching a town in a couple of miles."

"That would be nice unless you'd rather stay out of view, in which case I could fix something from the supplies Russell gave us."

"I'm unknown in this town, and like Russell pointed out, anyone looking for me won't be expecting a couple. It would be pleasant to sit in a café for a change and have a meal I didn't fix." Especially when doing it with a beautiful young lady.

"All right." She smiled, and the day seemed sunnier.

"It's settled then. I don't know Wellsville, but I'm sure they'll have a café."

"If they don't, we can always stop somewhere on the road."

"Good. Tell me how you came to work for a newspaper. Have you studied to be a reporter?"

She laughed. "Good heavens no. I'm just a typist there.

My goal is to become an author. I love to write, and I think I'm good at it. I've had a few articles published in papers and a short story in a women's magazine. But what I want to write is a novel."

"I'm impressed. Will you try for another job with a newspaper then?"

"Yes, although it takes away much of the time I need for writing. I'd love to do your brother's story. Maybe if I could get it published, it would help somehow."

"I'll think about it." Kirk said nothing more, and the conversation between them died.

He had significant reservations about publicizing Cage's dilemma. If his college learned he was a convicted bank robber, could it damage his grades or get him dismissed? Kirk feared the risks were too high. "He's my baby brother. Wouldn't you do all you can to help your little sister, if you had one?"

"Yes, but not everyone cares enough about their family to go as far as you've gone for Cage. I hope he knows how lucky he is to have you."

Kirk studied her. How did she understand the situation so well when they'd just met? It was as if she'd seen into his soul, heard the names he'd been called, smelled the rotten food thrown at him, felt the pain it caused, and cared enough to want to make his life a little better. Were he a normal man with a regular occupation, he'd jump at the chance to court her, but after hearing what other hangmen's families endured, he would never put anyone through that.

No, marriage wasn't for him.

They reached the town of Wellsville, and Adina saw that it was barely a town at all, consisting mostly of tents and prospectors, with few wooden buildings: a hotel that advertised as a café and saloon, two other saloons—one in a tent—and a general store.

Kirk stopped the wagon before the hotel, and Adina looked around. She'd never seen so many mud puddles and deep tracks on a public street.

"Well," he said, "it's not much, but at least we can get a meal here and maybe check out the store to see if they have any meat or food to add to our supply."

"All right. It's fortunate they're both on this side of the street. I wouldn't like trying to walk through that mud."

She slid off the seat and was already on the boardwalk when Kirk reached her, making her feel a little guilty as she saw his dismay at not helping her. And the mud his boots had collected from the street. "You should have gotten down on my side."

Ruefully, he studied his footwear. "You're right." He knocked and scraped as much off as he could. The one café in town adjoined a saloon inside the hotel. Miners in dirt-encrusted trousers and muddy boots lined the bar, along with a few business types in sack coats.

Adina couldn't wait to sit, study these strangers, and fantasize about their lives.

"You sure you want to eat here?" Kirk asked, his tone showing uncertainty.

"Why not? It might be educational." Adina loved it. There were some real characters in the room. "I love watching people and seeing how others live. This will help my writing."

He gave a reluctant frown and led her to a table at the back, as far from the bar as possible. They ate beef stew with cherry pie for dessert. Two men at the bar argued about the best way to locate gold, which Adina found fascinating, even when it turned into a fistfight.

Kirk quickly paid the bill, hurried her from the place,

and walked her to the store, keeping her to the inside with a protective arm around her waist. The Emporium mainly sold mining equipment and much of the ordinary stock used in such work. Their only meat was venison, which Adina declined to buy after one sniff. She chose cheese instead and some wonderful-smelling fresh bread. After storing their purchases in the wagon, they climbed back onto the seat and left town.

The more time she spent with Kirk, the more Adina liked him. He had an easy temperament, a pleasant laugh, and was easy to talk with. His manners were impeccable for a hangman who traveled in an inadequate tinker's wagon. But then, Kirk Reddick was more than a hangman; he was an educated preacher. She could easily envision him behind a pulpit before a vast, attentive congregation and wished she could hear him give a sermon. With his knowledge of the Bible, which he kept with him either inside the wagon or on the driver's seat, and his easy, pleasant manner and voice, she believed he would be an incredible minister. It made her admire him all the more.

They often fell into periods of silence, but she never felt uncomfortable, and he didn't seem to either. It just seemed natural. When Kirk showed signs of weariness in the afternoon, Adina insisted he nap. They found a spot to pull off the road, and she tucked him into bed, ignoring his protestations that he was okay.

"You're still recovering from a bullet wound, Kirk," she argued. "You need to let your body heal completely. You shouldn't even be driving a wagon. You should let me take a turn."

"You know I need to be in De Lamar in the morning, Adina." He resisted her efforts to cover him with a blanket. "Stop fussing over me."

"I like fussing over you." She meant it.

He gave in, and she went outside to jot notes in her journal about all she had seen and learned about people, including Kirk, and ideas in case she got to write about him and his brother, Cage. What an unusual name. She liked it but wondered how Kirk's parents had come up with it. Kirk, of course, was perfect for him, as a Kirk was a church in Scotland. She wondered if Cage's name came through his grandparents.

Sitting with her book on her lap and watching the clouds drift across the sky, she fantasized about what it would be like to marry Kirk and travel with him to preach in various towns instead of hanging people. Laughing at her own nonsense, she shook her head, closed her journal, and went inside to see if Kirk was awake.

She'd grown sleepy sitting in the sunshine, and the bed where he lay looked inviting. Kirk lay on the far side, turned toward the wall, and seemed to sleep soundly. There would be just enough room for her to lie beside him.

Did she dare?

She yawned for about the fourth time. Tossing caution to the wind, she locked the door and crawled onto the bed, careful not to wake Kirk. But the warmth he radiated felt so good she couldn't help cuddling a little closer. She'd have to stay awake to make sure she got up if he started to awaken.

Kirk's nose twitched as he slowly awoke, smelling something sweet and tempting, but when he went to turn over, something blocked his way. Cautiously, he peered over his shoulder, seeing two dainty legs and feet—mostly covered in a moss-green cotton print with tiny pink flowers—like Adina's dress.

Adina?

In his bed?

What was she doing here? Sleeping; that was apparent, but why? Didn't she realize how inappropriate it was? What if he'd thought he was dreaming and kissed her or did something even more shocking? Yet he loved seeing her there as if she belonged to him, belonged in his bed. If only she did.

Nudging her, he said, "Adina, wake up."

She stretched deliciously, and he cringed as his body reacted to the way she brushed against him. "Adina!"

Rolling onto her back, her eyes blinked open and looked at him. "Kirk?"

With a startled cry, she jumped from the bed. "Kirk, I can explain. I'm so sorry."

He clung to the blanket over his hips as if naked underneath, though only aroused. "You should be more careful. What if someone had come in and seen us like this?"

"Oh, I locked the door." She held her hands to her face, her eyes large and round like plates. "I came in to check on you. I was sleepy, and you looked so comfortable. There was...oh, that's no excuse. I have no excuse."

He almost chuckled; she was so flustered. Should he tell her he'd enjoyed finding her beside him? He wouldn't mind making it a regular habit. But if he told her, she'd likely be more horrified than right this minute.

Turning, she fled to the door, fumbled with the lock, and disappeared. Kirk helped himself to a glass of water before following. He found her standing beside the creek, staring into the gurgling water. He almost felt sorry for her; she appeared so shaken.

"Adina, there was no harm done. So, you took a nap with me while I slept. So what? Shall we get going? I am on a schedule."

He locked the cabin and climbed into the driver's seat. Adina joined him without speaking or meeting his gaze. Kirk got the mule moving, and a good hour of silence ensued until he saw movement up ahead. He watched until a rider on a buckskin horse came into focus. Unsure whether to pull off and hide in the trees, he said, "Someone's coming."

"Who? Can you tell?"

"No. Do you think we should get off the road? I don't want you in the middle of any trouble."

"What are you expecting?" she asked. "Someone who wants to stop the hanging in De Lamar?"

"You never know."

Something in the vicinity of the approaching rider's chest glinted in the sunlight. A gun barrel? Or a badge? It seemed the wrong shape and position to be a rifle. As he drew closer, Kirk decided it wasn't a weapon. "I think he might be a lawman."

"That would be a relief." Adina leaned closer, trying to see past the trees. "I see no hint that he means us harm. No gun in his hand."

"We'll soon learn his intent."

A few minutes later, the rider drew up next to them. He was young, around twenty, and bearded. "Howdy. I'm Deputy Henson. Might you be Mr. Reddick?"

Kirk eyed him with suspicion. "Why do you want to know?"

"Marshal Townsend of De Lamar sent me to escort y'all into town."

Relieved, Kirk nodded. "Thank you, and excuse me for doubting you for a moment there. I have to be so careful."

"I understand," Henson said. "There are a few strangers in town the marshal doesn't like the looks of. He's afraid they might be there to try to break the prisoner out or cause trouble somehow, so he wanted to make sure y'all didn't get lost or nothing."

"We'd appreciate the escort. I'm Kirk Reddick and this is Miss Kinnaird."

"Glad to meet you," he said in a Texas drawl that made Adina smile. He leaned over and offered his hand to Kirk, who shook with him. Henson wore spurs on his boots and sat on a Mexican-style saddle decorated with conchos.

"It was very nice of the marshal to send you," Adina said. "Especially if he might need you to help with those men."

Kirk suspected Adina enjoyed listening to the man and hoped to keep the conversation going. "Yes. You never know what to expect from the crowd at a hanging."

The deputy turned his horse around so he was riding alongside. "Well, we're prepared for anythin'. Marshal Sandford wired us 'bout the trouble y'all had in Red River. How are ya feeling? I can see your head's bandaged up 'n all."

"I'm fine. Still some pain, but that's it." He looked at Adina. "Miss Kinnaird has been an excellent nurse."

Deputy Henson grinned. "Lucky you to get such a pretty filly for a nurse."

"I think so. Is there a place where I can park this rig near the marshal's office or wherever your marshal plans to have the hanging?" Kirk asked. "I'd like to leave as quickly as possible afterward and not be seen by anyone other than you and the marshal."

Henson lowered his head, his brow furrowed as he considered his answer. "Don't have a gallows. Use a tree instead. It's outside the cemetery next to the church. Reckon ya kin park behind the church 'n come through the building to the hangin' tree, then go back the same way after."

"All right." Kirk nodded. "That sounds feasible."

"Follow me then."

They continued on, except that the deputy mostly stayed beside them, chattering.

"I'll bring the marshal to the church to meet you before he brings the prisoner down. I see ya be wearing a six-gun," the deputy said. "That's good, case'n there's trouble. Miss, you can wait in the church if'n ya like."

"Thank you." Adina smiled. "I imagine I'll do that. I don't care to see the hanging."

"Don't blame ya none for that," Henson said. "Town's just ahead. Reckon y'all can see the church spire through them quakies."

"Yes, I see it," Kirk said.

Later, they pulled up behind a good-sized stone building with a bell tower and spire. A house stood alongside. Beyond, the town consisted of a main street and a few side streets. Kirk parked by a door that led inside, probably to the minister's office.

Kirk had barely had the thought before a tall, gray-haired man emerged wearing a suit and a cleric's collar. Kirk's instant take was that the man had a strong character, decisive and authoritative.

"Welcome, sir," he said. "I see the deputy brought you the back way. It's a bit strange, but it's no problem. I'm assuming you're the man here to conduct the hanging?"

"That's right." Kirk climbed down and then helped Adina alight. He swiftly let go of her. Just seeing her did strange things to his heart. Touching her or being touched by her caused a zing to go through him. He wondered what kissing her would do. Likely cause his heart to stop completely. Even so, he'd love the opportunity. "I'm Kirk Reddick, and this is Adina Kinnaird, my nurse."

"Your nurse?" The reverend said the words with a hint of disbelief Kirk found annoying. Did he think he'd lied and Adina was his mistress or something else unsavory?

"I heard what happened at your last event," the man said. "It's a sad day when a man can't do his job without being shot at. I'm Reverend Davis. The woman on the porch next door is my wife."

She came down and joined them.

"How nice to have a nurse traveling with you. Would you like to come in and have some coffee or tea?" Mrs. Davis asked. "I prepare coffee for my husband, but I prefer tea. Come in, do."

"Thank you," Adina said. "That's very nice of you. A cup of coffee sounds lovely."

"Yes," Kirk added, though he wasn't sure he could like these people. Both seemed to be questioning Adina's relationship with him. "I could use one too."

"Reckon I'd best let Marshal Townsend know you're here," Deputy Henson said. "He'll be down to meet y'all soon."

Kirk thanked him, and the man rode off.

He and Adina followed Mrs. Davis into the house. The reverend brought up the rear. She took them into the kitchen, a large, comfy room with pretty cotton curtains on the windows and a big table. Everyone sat while she brought cups over and filled them with steaming coffee that smelled delicious.

"You have a lovely home, Mrs Davis," Adina said, sipping. She appeared to relish the flavor of the dark brew. "What is that beautiful vine growing just outside your door?"

"Oh, that's a clematis." The woman's voice showed her pride. "My sister still lives in England and sent it to me. I'm very fond of it and get abundant compliments when it's blooming."

"I can imagine. I've never seen anything more stunning. I love that blue color. It reminds me of morning glory, except the color is deeper, and the purple shade at the center sets it off beautifully."

"I agree." The woman sat across the table next to her husband. Despite the hint of disapproval regarding his traveling with Adina, they were friendly and pleasant. "My sister says the vine comes in all sorts of colors. I'm hoping she sends me others."

"Well, I'd love to keep in touch with you, if you don't mind," Adina said. "Maybe you can find out from your sister how I can get one if I ever get a house where I can plant it."

"Why, I'd be glad to. I'll write down our address before you leave." She turned to Kirk. "I understand you're here for the hanging, Mr. Reddick."

He felt slightly taken aback because she seemed unaware of the part Kirk would play in the event.

"That's true, Mrs. Davis. Besides being my nurse, Adina is a writer. She's going to write my story."

Mrs. Davis's eyes widened, and she appeared impressed. "Why, that's marvelous. What do you do, if I may ask?"

"Mavis," her husband said, "Mr. Reddick is the hangman."

The woman's eyes widened even more. "Oh, my."

As if Adina needed to ease the situation and fill in the sudden silence, she said, "It's an unusual profession, which Mr. Reddick does not enjoy. I felt it would make an interesting article for the newspaper I work for."

"And what newspaper is that?" Reverend Davis asked.

"The *Red River Weekly Review*. It's the paper for Red River Crossing." She reached under the table and laid her hand on Kirk's as if to give him solace or courage. Did she realize she was lying to a minister in front of another minister? He knew she was trying to help.

"I see." The preacher drank some of his coffee. "I would be interested in reading it when it appears."

"I'll send you a copy," Adina said. Another lie, since the paper's owner was dead.

A knock came on the door. Mrs. Davis rose to answer it and returned trailed by the deputy.

"We're ready for you, Mr. Reddick," he said.

Kirk set aside his coffee and rose. "Lead the way." He turned to the Davises. "Thank you for your hospitality."

Uncertain what to do, Adina rose also.

"I will see you to the door." Mrs. Davis popped up from

her seat and headed toward the entrance. "Must you leave as well, Adina? I'd love to visit with you longer."

Kirk turned toward her. "Stay, Adina. There's no need for you to come."

She looked at him with concern. "Oh, but—"

"I'll be all right." He put his hand on hers for an instant and followed the deputy to the door.

Mrs. Davis gestured for Adina to return to her chair. "Sit down, dear, and tell us more about the newspaper you work for."

Feeling dazed, she said, "No. Thank you, but I don't feel right letting Mr. Reddick face this alone. I'm going with him."

He started to argue with her, but the determination in her eyes stopped him. Instead, he put an arm around her waist and ushered her out the door. "I have to change into my costume. I think you should stay in the wagon."

"No, Kirk. I want to be close enough to help if you should need it."

He studied her for a second, sighed and slid an arm around her waist, taking her with him. He had to admit, just to himself, that it comforted him to have her close by.

They had no problem finding where the hanging was to take place. A crowd milled around a towering tree with a noose hanging from a low branch. A man sat on a horse underneath. Marshal Townsend stood a few feet away.

"Stay here." Kirk urged her into a gap between two columns at the front of the church. "As soon as it's over, I'll come for you, and we'll leave."

"All right," she said.

He turned in time to see a boy preparing to toss a tomato at him.

"Don't do that." Adina stepped in the way and scolded the boy. "That man is only doing his job, one he hates but has no choice in doing."

Kirk swallowed a smile at her tenacity in protecting him and went to do what he'd come for. No more than eighteen, a young man sat mounted on a bay horse under the noose, his hands tied behind him. "Hello," Kirk said. "I'm the hangman. Are you afraid, my son?"

The prisoner straightened. "Whadya you think, hangman?"

"I think it would be mighty unusual not to feel fear at what is ahead for you, and any man who denies being afraid is a coward. Do you believe in Jesus?" Kirk kept his voice low so no one else would hear.

The boy glanced around. "My ma always harped about that man, and I ignored her preaching." His voice lowered, the insolence gone. "Right now, I reckon he's up there waiting for me so he can deal out more punishment, likely send me to hell. Am I right?"

"It's been my understanding and belief that when we die, we're offered another chance to accept Jesus into our hearts, and God will take this into account, along with the depth of your guilt and regret for your sins. Do you accept Jesus into your heart?"

He shrugged his thin shoulders. "Yeah, I reckon. Why not?"

"Then bow your head and pray with me." Kirk bowed his head. "Heavenly Father, hear my plea. This boy has sinned but has accepted Jesus as his savior. I humbly ask that thee grant him mercy in the name of thy son, Jesus Christ. Amen."

He heard a faint *Amen* following his.

The crowd grew more boisterous, shouting for him to hurry and hang the outlaw. Pieces of rotten vegetables and fruit splattered everywhere, even on the horse, which grew restless and danced in place, held by the deputy.

"It's time," the marshal said. "Let's get this over with."

Kirk took the hood the lawman handed him, telling the boy, "I'm putting a hood over your head so that as you close your eyes, you'll see only those who await you in heaven, including the Father, the Son, and the Holy Ghost."

The young man softly cried as Kirk slipped the hood over his head along with the noose. Then he stepped back and swatted the horse's rump. It bolted free of the deputy's hold, only to be caught by a second, mounted deputy and brought back.

Kirk stopped the gentle swinging of the boy's body but left him hanging in place, knowing the onlookers wanted to see it. The other outlaw, mounted on his horse, gave Kirk a defiant glare as he approached him.

"What were you whispering to Billy, you murdering rat? Some sort of religious drivel? Well, don't try that on me. You can take your God and shove him where the sunlight won't find him. Ya hear me?"

This man was older, his face more brutal, eyes implacable. Without going any further, Kirk knew there was a hardened criminal. "God loves you, no matter how you defile his name. Regardless of what you've done here on Earth, he'll give you another chance to accept his wisdom when you reach the other side. My advice is that you take it. I'll put a hood over your head now so—"

"No! I ain't no sissy-pantsed coward who needs a hood. Let those sons o' dogs out there throw their garbage and yell what they want. I can take it. Let's just get this over with."

"Very well." He slipped the noose over the condemned man's head, stood back, and whacked the horse's rump.

And a second body swung in the wind, splattered with rotten food. Kirk turned to the marshal. "Will you send the document to the judge saying I performed as required, or do you want me to do it?"

"I'll take care of it on my way back to my office."

"Thank you."

"Sure."

Kirk went to fetch Adina, feeling disgusted and discouraged as always after such a distasteful chore. She saw him coming and hurried over, taking his hand as they rushed to the wagon behind the church, going around the minister's house rather than through it. They had a pretty good idea what the man and his wife thought of them and had no desire to see them again.

"Did the paperwork get sent to the judge giving you credit for a job done?" she asked.

"Yes."

They reached the wagon without problem, only to find the door open. Their possessions, supplies, bedding, even the mattress lay scattered over the ground.

And the mule's throat had been slit.

Chapter Five

"Oh, Kirk!" Adina ran to check on her sketchbook and journal. They lay tumbled among the other items. Some pages were damaged, but she saw nothing she couldn't fix or live without.

Kirk picked up his mattress and carried it inside. Gathering up his linens and blankets, she followed.

"I'll put clean sheets on," she said. "The blankets look all right. We could shake them to get rid of any bits of grass."

He turned from laying the mattress down and, saying nothing, took her into his arms. Not knowing what to do or expect, she put her arms around him and waited. He wasn't the only one who needed solace now. They stayed like that for several long moments. Finally, Kirk stepped back, his arms lowering to his sides.

"I apologize." He swiveled so that his side and back were to her. "The entire thing got to me for a minute there. Please excuse my lapse of decorum."

"Oh." She picked up a few of her clothes. "I'm sorry to hear you apologize. I felt honored to have you turn to me for comfort, especially since I needed a bit of the same myself. I'll clean this up."

"Adina," he said her name so softly she hardly heard it, and had there been a barely audible plea in his tone?

She faced him with hope in her heart, her pulse thudding. "Yes?"

"It's not easy for me to express feelings. After my brother's trial and having to become the hangman, I..." His voice trailed away.

Emotion filled Adina. Her chest tightened, and tears threatened. Love, she thought. Could she genuinely love this man? She put her arms around him. "Never fear exposing your feelings to me, Kirk. I care too much to ridicule or criticize you or anyone for what they feel. All I want is to help you, to solve your brother's dilemma, and free you from the noose you're tangled in."

She stepped back, but not before kissing his cheek. She

didn't get far from him afterward before he looped an arm around her and reeled her back into his embrace. He whipped off his hood, and his mouth came down on hers, and she returned the kiss a hundredfold.

Even after ending the kiss, he kept her in his arms. "You are the sweetest woman I have ever met." He followed the comment with a grin. "And you have the sweetest kiss as well."

"Kirk, you took me by surprise, but I'm glad you did. We haven't known each other long, but sometimes it doesn't take that much time to see the essence of a person and know you care for them."

"You're right. I've been thinking about how our situation looks to others, like the Davises. They're bound to think the worst. Because of this, we might consider a marriage of convenience. We might make it real when we get to know each other better. What do you say?"

Her eyes lit up, and she smiled. "How like you to think of that. You're so kind. I agree, it's a good idea. Shall we pay a visit to Reverend Davis after we get this mess cleaned up?"

"Sounds like a good plan." He picked up the coffee pot and a cup. "That's if he's willing to have anything to do with us."

Adina laid the things she'd accumulated in her arms inside the wagon. "You make a good point. Maybe we should go to the next town and visit the church there."

"I'd vote for that." He glanced around. "We have no idea who did all this, and I'd rather just forget about it."

After a moment, Kirk said, "Um, Adina, I should warn you that wives of hangmen aren't treated well by the public, and although I'd like to have children at some point, I worry about what they'd have to endure as well. So, I'd understand if you decide to annul it at some point."

Holding a blanket she'd been folding, she smiled. "I appreciate the warning, and I'll admit, I'm nervous about making a real commitment before we've gotten to know each other better, but I hope we can make it a real marriage at some point. I'd love to have children. We can't be sure you'll remain a hangman. Surely not forever. I believe we'll catch this man who framed Cage. Then you can become what you were meant to be: a preacher."

He took the few steps necessary to embrace her. "Adina, I've never been in love before, but I think if ever I could love anyone, it would be you."

"Thank you. You are so charming." She kissed him then, and he returned it, raising it to new heights that lasted several moments. Perhaps minutes.

Until a knock came on the open door.

Kirk released Adina from their kiss and looked out to see a man standing aside just enough not to see in. For an apparent reason—he'd already seen what was going on. Kirk couldn't help laughing. How delightful to be caught doing something as marvelous as kissing a woman—one about to become his wife. A week ago, he never would have believed this could happen.

Going to the door, he peered out at the deputy. Henson wore a gigantic grin.

"Spying on us, were you?" Kirk said, still smiling.

Deputy Henson laughed. "O' course not. I been looking for ya, but I'm thinking y'all might have something to tell me?"

"Actually, we do."

Adina joined him in the doorway, and he drew her close with an arm around her waist. "Adina has consented to become my wife. You're the first to know."

"Well, I'm more tickled than an army of frogs in a

pickle barrel, hearin' that." Henson stuck out his hand, and Kirk stepped down to shake it.

"Thank you," Kirk said.

"Yes. We appreciate your kindness." They joined the deputy on the grass.

Henson glanced around at the mess. "What happened here?"

"We found it like this when we returned from the hanging," Kirk told him.

"Except it was worse," Adina said, picking up a mixing bowl. "We put the mattress back on the bed, and I took in some of the bedding. It will all have to be washed, but I don't have the facilities for that here."

"Oh, hush puppies in a frying pan." Henson waved a dismissive hand. "Give it to me. There's an inexpensive, efficient Chinese laundry in town. Bundle up what you want washed, and I'll take it over. You'll get it back in one to two days."

Adina's eyes lit up. "That's unbelievable. Kirk, we need to do something for Deputy Henson to show our appreciation. He's been so good to us."

Henson held up his hands. "Don't y'all insult me with money. I won't take that. Can't as a lawman. I could be accused o' taking a bribe."

"I was thinking more along the lines of a nice supper tonight," she said.

He smiled. "Now, that's a reward even the devil hisself would enjoy. I don't get home-cooked meals often. I'm terrible at cooking my own self, and the café in town ain't precisely first-class."

Adina stepped back into the wagon. "I'll get the laundry ready now, and you can come back whenever you're ready. Supper will be served at six."

"Perfect." Henson looked at the goods still spread on the grass. "But let me help with this mess afore I go. Why don't you tell me where things go, and I'll take care of it."

"You've done so much for us already," Adina objected. "I'm sure you have deputy things you should be doing."

"Nope. Everything is wonderfully quiet, considering how matters went earlier. There won't be no drunks to lock up yet, so I'm free as a bird."

"If I weren't engaged to Kirk now, I'd come over there and kiss you," Adina said with a laugh. "On the cheek, of course."

"Lady, I've glimpsed you kissing, so even getting that would put me in Heaven."

They all laughed.

"My, but you're good at exaggeration," Adina said.

"You could pick up all the obvious kitchen things and put them inside the doorway so I can wash them. That would help a lot."

"Will do." The deputy went straight to work.

That allowed Kirk to gather harness equipment to store under the wagon until they could get another animal. "I don't want to take advantage of you, Henson, but where would a man go to buy a mule or horse around here, and how can I dispose of a dead one?"

"By gum, I forgot about that." Henson straightened from picking up tin plates and cups. "Noticed the mule earlier. Now, that's something for a deputy to investigate. The rest of this is bad enough, but whoever did that should be in jail. Y'all want me to take care of that now or finish this?"

"Give Adina what you're holding and see about the mule, please. You're right; it should have been reported to the marshal immediately."

Adina appeared in the doorway and accepted the kitchenware Henson held up to her. "I had forgotten about that poor creature," she said. "He was a good, obedient little beast, too."

Henson walked over to the carcass, studied the slit neck, and looked around for clues.

Kirk watched and felt terrible, realizing he should have

gone to the law before going near the wagon. They may have obliterated evidence that would have helped the deputy. Kirk would make a point now of studying the ground and items before he picked them up to put away. If they could catch the culprit, they might be able to get them to pay for a new mule at least. That would help. Kirk didn't carry a lot of cash on him. Too much chance of being robbed. As a hangman, he was more vulnerable to thievery than the average man on the road. He kept his funds in a good national bank with offices in most cities and many towns. But he doubted there would be one in this little burg, so he hoped a new mule wouldn't be too expensive should he have to pay for one.

"Ah," Henson exclaimed. "I found a good clue, a track I recognize that looks recent. I'm going to check it out. I'll see you later."

"Good luck, Deputy," Adina called from the wagon.

Kirk walked over to the door. "We have most of it done, don't we?"

"Yes. The deputy was very helpful."

"Would you like me to walk you to the stream to wash those dishes?"

"That be nice, Kirk." She stuffed the last cup into the pillowslip she used to hold everything and stepped out of the wagon.

Kirk locked it before taking the pillowslip from her and carrying it to the stream. "I wonder if this meets up with a river. Seems like most do eventually."

"Except in dryer country." She kneeled beside the pillowslip and took out the first dish. "Then sometimes, they simply dry up and cease to be."

"Yes. It's sad when there is so much need for water in those areas."

"Kirk?"

He recognized Henson's voice coming from far away, probably the wagon. "Over here," he shouted, waving an arm. Henson started toward them. Adina began washing dishes, setting them on a towel afterward.

The deputy had brought another man, who looked somewhat dejected, his shoulders slumped and his head hanging. He looked guilty. Kirk's hopes soared. "Deputy Henson, you returned quicker than expected."

"I brought someone to see you. This is Arthur Keegan. He has something he wants to say."

"Uh, yes." Arthur shuffled his feet nervously. "It, uh, it was me who ransacked your wagon, and I apologize. It was wrong of me to do that. I'm sorry."

"We very much appreciate hearing that, Mr. Keegan,"

Kirk said. "I hope you realize now that I was only doing a job, one I can assure you I take no pleasure in and only do because the law ordered it."

Keegan glanced at Henson. "The deputy explained about you not having a choice about being a hangman. Are you really doing this so your brother won't have to?"

"That's true. My brother was framed for bank robbery, and the judge gave Cage a choice of prison or being the hangman. I believed prison might well kill my brother as he doesn't have a strong constitution, so I asked to take his place. This way, he can attend college and learn to become a lawyer."

"By gum, sir, you deserve a medal for that. I'm doubly sorry for what I done. I'll pay for the mule. Always considered 'em useless critters myself, but some folks like 'em."

"Mules have more endurance than most horses," Kirk told him. "They are cheaper to buy, easier to feed when traveling, and do better on the rough ground I often encounter on country roads."

Keegan's eyes widened, and he appeared impressed. "What do ya know? I'm gonna remember that."

The deputy held out a few bills and some gold coins. "He came up with this. I talked with Sal over at the stable; he has a horse he'll sell you for this amount. I looked the mare over pretty well, and I think it's a good deal."

Kirk took the money and stuffed it in his pocket without counting it. "I'm very grateful, Mr. Keegan."

"I'm only sorry I don't have more. The wife, she handles the money. Keeps me on a tight budget, I'll tell you. Only gives me a bit at a time. She's smart. If'n I had all my earnings, I'd just spend 'em at the saloon."

"If this buys us a good horse to replace the mule, it will be all we need. Thank you again," Kirk said and shook hands with the man.

Keegan nodded and looked at Henson, who jerked his head, indicating that the man could go. Keegan wasted no time disappearing.

"Deputy Henson," Kirk said. "You've done it again. We are deeply in your debt."

"Fiddlesticks. Just doing my job is all, and I'm looking forward to eatin' with y'all tonight."

"How did you know who'd done it?"

Henson grinned. "That was easy. The track I saw had a nail sticking out of the heel kinda crooked like, and I'd noticed a few days ago that Keegan left a similar print." His gaze wandered toward a man walking toward them. "Maybe ya could say a few words to put my boss at ease."

The marshal strolled toward them. "Mr. Reddick, I understand you experienced a bit of trouble."

Before Kirk could answer, Henson added, "Marshal Townsend was pretty upset to hear what happened."

"That's right," the lawman said. "Don't like such happenings in my town."

"Well..." Kirk offered his hand, and the marshal accepted. "Everything has been put to rights now, sir. Deputy Henson here has been invaluable in helping us. He's a good man."

"That's why I hired him." The aging man slapped Henson on the back. "Glad to hear all is okay here. I'll mosey back to my office then. Got some wanted posters to go through."

"Good luck with them," Kirk said.

When the lawman vanished around a corner, Henson turned back from watching him. "Going through wanted posters is his favorite part of his job."

Kirk laughed. "I hope he has luck capturing them. Do him some good."

"Yeah." Henson frowned. "'cept it'll be me he'll send after 'em. Never leaves town himself."

Kirk sobered. "That seems unfair."

"Not much about life that is fair, is there?"

Chapter Six

"Where do you have to be next?" Adina asked as they drove out of De Lamar two days later with the new sorrel mare pulling the wagon. She was glad to be leaving. Having their home-on-wheels raided had been unpleasant and taken a lot of work to get back in order. Plus, cooking a special dinner for Deputy Henson, though he seemed to enjoy it.

"I was going to talk to you about that. I checked this morning and don't have to be in Flint until next week. That means this would be a good time to get married and get to know each other better."

Adina's heart leaped at that idea. Suddenly, she became nervous. Kirk had been through so much and deserved a good life. Could she make him happy? But she couldn't let him see her doubts. "That sounds wonderful, Kirk. So where shall we go for this happy event?"

"I was thinking Silver City. They have a nice hotel there, and sleeping in a real bed for a change would be nice. There's a pharmacy, too, and I need more of my sleeping tablets."

"Sleeping tablets? Those can't be good for you. Surely, there are better ways to help you sleep."

"Like what?" he asked.

"I could sing lullabies to you." She grinned.

He glanced at her, surprise on his handsome face. "You can sing?"

"I'll let you be the judge." It seemed a perfect day for singing as they crossed a beautiful meadow alive with birds and bright with wildflowers. Opening her mouth, she began the lyrics of Aura Lea: "*When the blackbird in the spring, on the willow tree sat rocked, I heard him sing, singing Aura Lea. Aura Lea.*"

As she sang, Kirk reached over and laid his hand on hers on her lap. She turned her hand over and gripped his, still singing.

When she finished, he leaned over and kissed her

cheek. "That was beautiful, Adina. You should be on a stage, but I'd be crazy to encourage you to do that because then I'd lose you."

"Maybe not," she said. "Besides, I have no interest in singing on a stage. I used to take part in the church choir. I probably will again once I settle down. Singing professionally seems a terrible life, traveling to new places almost daily and eating only restaurant food. Everyone they know wants something from them. They have no real friends."

Kirk said nothing for a few minutes. "Adina, do you realize you just described my life? Yet here you are, sharing that life with me and discussing marriage."

She leaned over and kissed him. "Yes, but we are friends, so I won't be without them, and we don't eat restaurant food every day either. No one wants anything from me, and I have a chance to write a great tale."

"You mean Cage's?"

"No. The life of a hangman," she answered.

"What about Cage's story?"

"Won't it all come down to the same thing?" She laughed. "Cage's story leads into yours. And I probably won't use real names. I'll fictionalize it to make it more exciting."

He grinned. "Getting shot, having gangs after me, getting the wagon vandalized—my life isn't exciting enough?"

"Depends on how it's written. Don't worry." She squeezed his hand. "When it's done, I'll send a copy to the judge explaining that it's about Cage and you. I want to get it published, but I'm enough of a realist to know that it may take a while. A long while. Maybe forever. Getting published isn't easy, especially for a woman."

She eyed him speculatively. "Maybe I should use your name as the author."

Kirk chuckled. "That should amuse everyone who knows me. Cage in particular."

"Entertainment is the purpose of fiction, love."

"You could use A. Reddick. Then they won't know you're a woman."

"Excellent idea." Up ahead, Adina saw movement. Keeping her eyes on the spot, she watched until her excellent vision made out half a dozen riders coming toward them.

Beside her, she felt Kirk tense, and the horse slowed.

"Tell me, Kirk, do you happen to have a rifle?"

"I have two. One beneath the seat and one inside. You see the riders too, eh?"

"Yes. I think you need to stop for a minute." She hoped

he understood what she intended. They didn't have time to discuss it.

He reined in, and she jumped down, letting herself into the wagon.

The sound of horses galloping up came from outside, then a man's voice. "Howdy. You wouldn't happen to be the county hangman, would you?"

Kirk answered, "Why? You want somebody hanged?"

"Just the opposite," a second voice said, his tone harsh and angry. "He's figuring to hang a couple of our friends in Flint next week."

"We only want to talk to him," the first man said more calmly.

An idea popped into Adina's head. She set aside the rifle, gathered the new kitchen utensils they'd bought, and stepped outside. "Hello, gentlemen. If you're looking for some kitchenware to please your wives, you've come to the right place. Would you like me to show you—"

"What the devil? That ain't what we want," a man growled. None of them looked like gentlemen, more like saloon dregs.

"She your wife?" asked another man she judged to be the best of the lot. They were after trouble, nothing else.

Her mind scrambled for the best way to disarm the situation.

"Husband, what's going on here?" she asked in a whiny voice. "I think I'd better go back in the wagon."

"Good idea, lady. Who are you, mister?" the lead man asked.

"We're tinkers," Kirk answered. "We sell kitchenware to farmers and stores. We're on our way now to Silver City. I promised the wife a night in the hotel there."

"You ain't going to Flint?" a gruff voice asked.

"No. I just told you we're going to Silver City," Kirk said. "You sure you wouldn't like to see some fine utensils or maybe a new frying pan for the wife? We just got some new cookware in and—"

"We ain't interested, I tell ya."

Pride rose inside Adina at how Kirk remained calm and sounded like a salesman. He had quickly picked up on her sham. She ran her fingers idly over the rifle's metal barrel while waiting to see if Kirk needed backing up. He was a good, intelligent man. For now, a marriage of convenience was a fine idea, but she wasn't so sure she didn't want a real marriage. Her attraction to the man grew daily.

"He isn't the hangman, Davey, or he wouldn't have a wife. Let's go."

"I dunno. Maybe we should—"

"Elmer's right, Davey-boy, we're wasting our time here."

"Okay. Okay."

The next sound Adina heard was horses trotting off the direction she and Kirk had come from. She left the wagon and climbed into her seat next to the man she was coming to love. "You handled that so well, Kirk. I'm proud of you. You should have been an actor on a stage."

His laughter filled her with joy and had her laughing, too.

"Me!" he said. "You were the one who did the trick. I didn't know what you had in mind when you had me stop and went inside. I half expected you to come out toting the rifle like Annie Oakley."

Adina had to bend over; she was laughing so hard. "Oh, this is exhausting. Let's get to Silver City and that lovely hotel you mentioned. I need a nap."

"A grand idea." With a flick of the reins, he had the horse moving again.

"I'm going to name the horse Brownie," she said.

"Sound like a fine name to me. I never named the mule."

"Well, I miss not having a pet. I usually have a cat. I

love them. Since we don't have one, I thought I'd make Brownie my pet. Maybe I'll see if I can find a cat in Silver City to adopt. I saw a mouse running out of a cupboard when we were cleaning up."

"I hope it left. I detest the little varmints. But if you want a cat, that's fine with me. I like them, too."

"You're so good to me, Kirk. Thank you."

"You're welcome. I find that I like pleasing you."

She hugged his arm.

After a moment of silence, she said, "There's something else I've been wondering about. Do you think we'll both be able to sleep in that bed after we're married? It's rather small."

"I had the same concern, so I was thinking of seeing if there might be a covered wagon for sale somewhere." He picked up her hand from her knee and kissed the back. "You see them parked in farmer's fields now and then. We could watch for one."

"I love that idea. It would give us much more room. I had thought about a sheepherder's wagon. They have stoves and lots of storage space. I worried about how big the bed would be, though."

"A sheepherder's wagon might work, but like you said—" He shook his head.

"Maybe we could get a carpenter to adjust it," she said, with hope in her voice. "Sort of a fold-down bed. It would be so nice to have a stove."

"Yes, not having to cook over a fire would be a real advantage, and the stove would heat the wagon. We couldn't keep it going all the time, of course. Too much fire danger."

"We'd have to be vigilant, just like having a stove in a house, except worse."

He laid her hand back on her knee and patted it before returning to the reins. "I trust you would handle it well."

"I feel confident we can do it." She watched the landscape slowly slide by: trees, wildflowers, and an open space where a deer and fawn grazed. She loved seeing wild animals. Some big cities were building zoos to keep animals where people could view them safely, but she felt sorry for the creatures being held captive. They had a right to be free as God intended.

How likely were they to find a sheepherder's wagon for sale? She doubted many would be available. They might have to find a carpenter who could build one.

She looked at Kirk, admiring how his hair curled over his collar. It was longer than most men wore, but she liked it that way. He'd surprised her the way he'd kissed and held her hand. Such a sweet gesture and something she'd expect from a man who truly loved his wife and had been with her a while. Not at all like her situation, which made it more precious.

They arrived in Silver City an hour before suppertime. By the time they'd arranged with the livery for the wagon and horse, they found the lobby of the Idaho Hotel crowded with avid folks waiting for tables in the restaurant. Luckily, the check-in desk was open, so they arranged for rooms, checked them out, and left their spare clothes inside. By the time they descended the stairs again, they could enter the restaurant. The food proved tasty, but Adina was yawning before they returned to their rooms.

After a good night's sleep, they enjoyed baths before having a good breakfast. While waiting for the livery boy, Billy, to finish hitching the horse to the wagon, they explored the town. When they returned, Adina asked if Billy knew of any sheepherder's wagons for sale.

The boy scratched his head while he searched his brain. Being tall and lanky, he towered over Adina and stood nearly as tall as Kirk, but while his bare arms showed good musculature, he wasn't as strong as Kirk. His ragged clothes caused her to worry about whether he had a good home, and she wished she could find out. She couldn't ask him.

"I can't think of any," he said finally, "but I do know a good carpenter who's done some for a couple of sheepmen I know. Did a good job, too. His name is Ivan Kingsman. Nice guy."

She and Kirk smiled at each other. How lucky they were to have found a carpenter so easily. Kirk asked Billy for directions to find the man. Twenty minutes later, they were discussing wagon designs with Kingsman. He seemed to know what he was doing and had a wagon half-finished to show them his skill.

"Can you start with the wagon I have now, or do you need to start fresh?" Kirk asked.

Ivan walked to the tinker's wagon and looked it over, mainly studying the axle and base. "I think it would be best if I started from scratch."

When he straightened to his full height, Adina figured he might well be the tallest man in town and the tallest she'd ever seen, even taller and heavier than Kirk.

"What I believe you want," he continued, "needs a longer, wider and stronger axle. The next question is how you want the top. On a typical pioneer wagon, it's rounded, but I can make it square. I think the rounded top allows the wind to flow over them more easily, which is likely why pioneers used that design. With the square design, you'd have to worry about wind toppling it over."

"Sounds reasonable to me," Kirk said. "Let's go with the rounded one but make the rig as long as possible. This will be our home for much of the year, so we need as much room as possible."

"Yes," Adina added. "And can you put windows in? I'd love to be able to see out."

"I've done that before. I can put one on each side and one at the end so you can open it and talk while you're inside and he's driving." He rubbed his bristled chin, which hinted he hadn't shaved that morning. "Of course, you lose cupboard space that way. A square top might be better for you after all, as I could put in more cupboards to make up for the windows. I think it would be all right if you're not traveling long distances and are unlikely to be caught in a bad windstorm. Maybe give the corners a bit of a slant to help the wind blow over. I can also make the door with a small window so you can see anyone who knocks before opening it."

Excited, Adina couldn't help bouncing on her heels a little. "Oh, that sounds perfect, doesn't it, Kirk?"

"I agree." He slid an arm around her waist.

"The windows can be small," Ivan said. "Why don't you let me fiddle with the design and see what I can come up with?"

"That might be best," Kirk said. "How long would the construction take? I need to be in another town in a few days, but I can return afterward."

Ivan leaned back against his worktable and frowned as he stared into space, presumably computing the time it would take to have the wagon ready. He had big hands and muscles everywhere, evidence of his hard work. Blond hair fell across his forehead, which he often pushed out of the way. "If I don't get distracted by orders for caskets that are needed right away, I think I can have it done in two weeks. Usually, it takes me closer to a month, but I know you need this to live in, so I'll rush it."

Kirk nodded and smiled. "That would be mighty fine of you. We'd greatly appreciate it."

"Yes," Adina added, thrilled by the carpenter's words. "We'll find a way to work our schedule around yours if necessary. We'll be all over the county."

"You never leave the county?" Ivan asked.

Adina looked at Kirk, afraid suddenly that she'd said too much. They had to be so careful not to give too much information about what Kirk did for a living.

He didn't lose his smile, however. "We can. In my work, I can pretty much go where we want."

"You're a tinker, isn't that right?" He scratched his

head. "I've never thought I could do that kind of work, but it wouldn't be so bad if you could bring your wife along. Some men would be glad to get away from home now and then, but not me. I never tire of my family."

"I think I'd be the same way." Kirk gave Adina an affectionate look. "I've been alone most of my life. I asked Adina to marry me partly because of her willingness to travel with me. It doesn't make much sense to get a wife and then go off and leave her all the time."

"I agree." Ivan pushed away from the table. "Well, I'll get to work right away on your rig. You came at an opportune time, one of the rare moments when I don't have any orders to fill besides the one I showed you that's half-done. I do have to finish that one."

"That was lucky." Kirk held out his hand, and the men shook. "We'll check back with you before we leave town to see how it's going and find out when to return."

"All right," Ivan said. "I'll see you then."

As they strolled back to the hotel, Adina took his hand as they walked. "Sounds like all we have to do now is decide what we want to do here in Silver City."

"I know. It's a delicious notion. Seems like all I do is travel, hang someone, travel, hang a man, and travel some more."

"I can understand why you'd find that tiring, Kirk, but at least you're not alone anymore."

"Yes, and isn't that a treat?" He leaned over and kissed her cheek. "I can honestly tell you that I've been happier since you joined me than I've been in a long time."

"Oh, Kirk, I'm so pleased. I've enjoyed our time together, too, and before I met you, I wasn't the least interested in getting married. I just wanted to write."

"You can write all you want now." He smiled and opened the hotel door. "What do you say we have some of the restaurant's wonderful pie?"

"That sounds heavenly. I think I'll try the coconut. I never would have thought of putting coconut in a cream pie, but it sounds intriguing, doesn't it?"

He chuckled. "I'm more interested in the apple pie, and it's made with fresh fruit, not last fall's crop, kept in a cellar all winter."

They crossed the lobby and were about to enter the restaurant when a man in a leather coat shoved open the exit half of the double doors and bumped into Adina, nearly knocking her to her knees. She uttered a brief cry of surprise and alarm but caught her balance.

"Careful there, Mister," Kirk said to the stranger as he reached to help her. "You almost knocked my companion here down."

The man turned and glared at Kirk, paying no attention whatsoever to Adina, for which she was thankful.

"How about I knock you down?" the man snarled.

"No, thank you," Kirk replied, turning his attention to Adina.

She accepted his help but took her time straightening and hid behind him. When the man stormed outside, she said, "Kirk, that was the man who killed my boss, Jason."

Chapter Seven

"Are you sure that was the killer?" Kirk stepped toward the door the man had just gone out through.

"Yes. I'll never forget his face. I got a very close look at him through the window in the door. It's him, all right. Let's go tell the town marshal."

Kirk's attention centered on the hotel check-in desk. "Just a moment."

He walked over, and the clerk looked up. "Did you see that man who just left?" Kirk asked.

The clerk glanced at the door. "The one in the leather coat?"

Kirk nodded. "Yes. Do you know him?"

"As a matter of fact, he's a guest." The clerk pulled over

a notepad. "Would you like to leave a message for him?"

"Not now. Can you tell me how long he'll be here?"

"Yes, he's reserved his room for two more days."

"Good. I'll see him around then and can talk to him in person."

Kirk rejoined Adina, who was peering out the oval windows in the front doors. She turned when he touched her arm. "There's no doubt, Kirk. He just rode away on the horse I saw outside the newspaper office that day."

"He's staying here and will be for two more nights, so we have time to notify the marshal."

"Good." She hooked her arm through his, and they hurried to the jail.

Inside, they found the man they sought at his desk reading a paper. "Hello. I'm Marshal Green. Is there something I can do for you folks?"

"Yes," Adina said. "A man is staying at the Idaho Hotel, and I know without doubt that he murdered the man I used to work for in Red River Crossing."

The marshal frowned. "Why don't you sit down?"

They sat in chairs opposite the lawman. "I can give you a description of him and his horse," Adina said.

"That would be helpful," Green answered. "I read something recently about a murder in Red River Crossing.

A newspaperman, if I remember right."

"Yes. Jason Johanson." Adina nodded, perched on the edge of her chair. "I was downstairs at the time, and Jason—my boss—was in his apartment overhead. I heard thuds and voices arguing and became worried. Then I heard a gunshot. I decided I should flee and get the marshal. When I reached the door, the man I just saw at the hotel was coming down the stairs. I hurried out and locked him inside. He yelled at me from the other side of the window in the door, so I had a perfect view of him. And there was a strange horse outside. I shooed it away, hoping to slow the killer down so Marshal Sandford could catch him, but it didn't work. The murderer escaped."

"Until now," said the marshal across from them.

"Yes." Adina grinned. "Until now."

"Before coming over here," Kirk added. "I checked with the hotel clerk and learned the man is expected to stay a couple more days."

"Excellent. Where is he now?"

"He rode off on his horse," Adina said. "You can't mistake it, a black gelding with a white face and a black cross in the white. The saddle blanket is red. It stands out against his black coat."

"Where are you headed next?" Green asked.

Adina looked at Kirk.

"Back to the hotel, I guess," he said.

Green rose from his chair. "I'll walk over with you to get the killer's room number and name."

"I hope his room isn't near ours," Kirk said.

They learned the room was number ten, down the hall and on the other side of the stairs from Kirk and Adina, much to their relief. They also got a name: Sam Smith. Fake was the marshal's conclusion.

Green left to search for the black horse with the red saddle blanket, and Kirk and Adina went to the restaurant for their pie. Later, they found the pharmacy, and Kirk got the needed sleep tablets.

They got a good night's sleep and attended church since the following day was Sunday. After the service, they waited until everyone was gone to speak to the preacher in privacy. Kirk introduced himself, not as Kirk Reddick, the hangman, but as Kirk Reddick, the minister, who wished to be married to the young woman at his side.

"Why, I'm delighted to meet another preacher, and I love doing weddings," the middle-aged man said. He had premature gray hair and the whitest teeth Adina had ever seen. His voice made her wish to hear him sing. "I'm Pastor Jones. When would you like to do the deed?"

Kirk looked at her, and she shrugged. "Anytime."

"The bride already has her wedding gown?" Jones asked.

Adina crinkled her nose and shook her head. "I wouldn't have anywhere to wear or store a wedding gown, and I don't need one."

"Now that isn't true," Kirk argued. "You don't have to buy a fancy gown, but you should have a new one. In fact, I insist, and I'm buying."

"Well..." She grinned. "In that case, and since I'm unemployed now, I accept."

Kirk turned from Jones to Adina. "Why don't we see if there are any shops here with ready-made dresses and have the ceremony this afternoon before I leave for Flint?"

Adina's brow furrowed. "I don't see that advantage since I'm going with you."

Kirk shot Jones a glance as if embarrassed she'd contradicted him. "We'll discuss that later. What do you think, Reverend Jones? Will today be a good day for you?"

"It will be perfect," he said, smiling broadly.

"All right, then we're going shopping." Kirk took Adina's hand and started down the church steps.

Pastor Jones followed to the entrance. "There's a shop called Glory's Needle across from the butcher where my wife likes to shop. You might try there."

"We'll do that."

As they hurried toward the exit, Adina stopped suddenly, struck by the beauty of a painting of Jesus on the back wall.

"What is it?" Kirk asked.

"That painting is so well done." She turned toward the Pastor. "Who did this picture?"

"Why, my wife did it. She's quite the artist, isn't she?" Jones said, joining them.

"Indeed, she is," Adina said. "I've never seen a better portrait of our savior."

"I agree," Kirk added. "You have a talented wife, Pastor."

"I know." The pride in his voice rang clearly through his simple words.

"We'd better go." Kirk tugged at Adina, and they left the church, aiming for the main thoroughfare.

"What a lovely man." Adina took Kirk's arm. "I'd love to meet his wife. You know, Kirk, I greatly like Silver City. It seems a perfect place to live."

"It is nice. Perhaps if we can catch the man who framed Cage someday, we'll be able to settle somewhere like this."

He appreciated that she didn't argue. It meant that she

understood he had no choice but to be the hangman. She was wonderfully cooperative and always seemed eager to please him. It made him glad to make her happy. He felt optimistic about the future of their marriage.

"Shall we look for Glory's Needle?" Kirk asked when they reached Jordan Street.

"Might as well. My appointment calendar is open for the rest of the day."

He chuckled at her joke. Adina's calendar was always open.

They found the store right where the preacher said it would be, the wooden edifice a color between blue and lavender, with a fair-sized window displaying charming clothing and accessories. A bell jingled when they entered, and a graceful young woman emerged from a back room. She wore a unique gown that flattered her figure and, Kirk assumed, displayed her design talent.

"Hello," she said. "Can I show you anything, or are you browsing?"

"We need a special dress for our wedding," Kirk said.

"How exciting. Congratulations." The slender store owner had hair the color of honey twisted on the back of her head with a decorative, beaded comb holding it in place. "Is Pastor Jones doing the honors?"

"Yes, this afternoon," Adina said. "I don't want anything too fancy, though. Kirk is a traveling salesman, and we'll be living in a wagon, so I'll be cramped for storage space and need something to wear to other events."

"You only get married once, you realize," the woman said. "But I understand. I'm Glory, by the way, and I own the place. Let's see what I can find for you in a ready-made." She turned to Kirk. "There's a chair over there if you'd like to wait."

He glanced out the window. "I think I'll go do some exploring. What time should I come back?

"In about an hour, I should say."

"Very well. Don't let her scrimp on money. I'm buying and want my beautiful bride's gown to be as beautiful as she is."

"Oh, I'll happily see to that." The girl laughed.

After Kirk left, she became more serious. "What shall I call you, and what do you have in mind for your bridal dress?"

"Well, call me Adina." She surveyed the goods on display. Glory sold accessories and dresses in an excellent variety. "My favorite color is purple, so maybe something lavender? And, like I said, nothing too fancy, no matter what that man said."

"Most of my ready-to-wears are my designs and sewn by my hand, which means they're cheaper than those shipped in. Oddly enough, I'm also fond of purple, so I have several in that color."

She led the way to a rack of dresses and pulled out one of a shade between purple and lavender, similar to the paint on the building. Adina liked the color but not the design. "It's a little low-necked for me."

Glory studied it. "I might be able to fix that, but let's look at others first. How about this one?"

This time, she selected a more demure dress close to the same shade but with a higher, heart-shaped neckline and buttons down the front.

"Oh, I like that one very much. The neckline is romantic, don't you think?"

Glory chuckled. "Yes, that's why I made it that way. The skirt won't need many petticoats or crinolines, so it won't require a lot of room in your closet."

"I love how the skirt folds back to reveal the ruffles and that gorgeous short train." Adina couldn't resist touching it and found the fabric as soft as it looked.

"It's brushed broadcloth," Glory said. "It looks like velvet but is much cheaper and easier to clean."

"I don't think we need to look further," Adina said,

then frowned. "Unless this one doesn't fit me."

"Let's find out, shall we?"

Glory led her to a dressing room in a curtained-off section. Adina went to work, removing her outfit. Once she was down to her shift and corset, Glory lifted the gown over Adina's head, careful not to muss the curls Adina had painstakingly arranged on the back of her head. She worked the upper buttons while the shop owner did those on the skirt. When their fingers met, Glory stepped back, allowing Adina to see herself in the full-length triple set of mirrors on the back wall.

She gasped with pleasure. The gown looked as if made for her.

"It couldn't fit better if I'd sewn it to order," Glory said.

"Yes, it's perfect, isn't it?" Adina checked the back and liked how it appeared. "Honestly, Glory, I love it. I couldn't ask for anything more beautiful."

"I'm so pleased you like it. What we need now is a hat, gloves, and shoes. I can provide the gloves, but I'm not sure about the shoes, although I do keep some in stock. Do you want long gloves or short? Short, I'm thinking."

She went to a cabinet full of shallow drawers and returned with purple kid gloves.

"Oh, how wonderful." Adina instantly pulled them on.

Next, Glory left the room, returning with a hat that won a gasp of pleasure from Adina. It matched the dress's color perfectly. Purplish-blue morning glory blossoms circled the brim as if grown there, and a veil draped down to partially cover the face.

"That is the most exquisite hat I've ever seen." Adina reached for it.

Glory let her admire it for a few moments. "Let me put it on so you can see how it goes."

Adina handed it back and watched in the mirror while Glory set it on her head so that it sloped upward in the back to display the mass of curls arranged there. The shop owner drew a single thin curl free to hang down Adina's cheek.

"It is even more elegant on you with that gown," Glory said. "Look at you. Never have I seen a more stunning bride."

Adina studied herself critically, turning this way and that to see every side of her in the three-way mirror. She saw no flaw. Turning to Glory, she grinned. "You've created a miracle. I've never looked this good in my life."

"You're still very young. Stick with me, and you could become the grand dame of Silver City.

Laughter trickled out of Adina, pleasure over Glory's

statement and embarrassment.

At that moment, Kirk called from the outer room, "Adina, are you there?"

"Yes, Kirk. I'll be out soon. I just need to change." Adina fumbled with the buttons.

"Don't change if you're wearing what you wish to be married in, Adina. Remember, the preacher is waiting to perform the ceremony."

"Oh, yes." She began rebuttoning.

Glory stepped over and put a hand over Adina's trembling ones. "Relax, dear. The minister will wait. This is your wedding day, a joyous occasion. No need for nerves. Besides, we haven't found shoes for you yet."

Adina gave her an uncertain smile and tried to calm herself. It wasn't as easy as it sounded.

Her wedding day. *Oh, my. And tonight will be our wedding night.*

Her anxiety doubled, then tripled.

She looked at Glory and whispered, "I don't know if I can do this."

Glory smiled. "Of course, you can. You're marrying a very handsome and caring man. I saw that right off. You have nothing to worry about. Here." She pointed to a stool, picked up a teapot, and poured a pale brown liquid into a lovely cup. "Sit carefully so you don't wrinkle the skirt and drink this."

She gently pushed Adina onto the stool and handed her the cup and saucer. "I will check the back to see what shoes I can find."

When she returned, she carried three boxes. "I should have asked what size you wear before I checked the back."

Adina looked at the size printed on the end of a box. "Oh, these should work."

"Good. I found three shades of purple in three styles." She took the shoes out and lined them up in a row. The first pair were tall with frilly lace along the lace-up placket and high heels. The second pair were ankle boots with a low heel and a deeper purple brocade on the upper part. The third pair were high button boots in deep purple velvet.

"I like these." Adina picked up the middle pair and drew up her skirt to try them on.

"Here." Glory took them from her. "Let me."

"Oh, they fit." Adina stood and took a few steps. "They even feel comfortable."

"And they go perfectly with your dress," Glory added.

"I think I'm ready to be married."

"Indeed, you are. Have some more tea while I take care

of the financial end of this purchase with your fiancé, and then we'll show him what he's paying for."

"He might be more willing to hand over the cash if he sees me first," Adina said. "That's if I look as good as you've claimed."

Glory laughed. "You do, and you have a business head on you. Shall we see if your idea works?"

Adina nodded. What was she so concerned about? She adored Kirk. She wanted to be his wife. It was what would happen in their marriage bed tonight she felt uncertain about. Her mother had explained how babies came to be and made it sound amazing. But Adina wasn't ready for motherhood yet, and the process of getting there sounded awkward and embarrassing.

Glory went to the curtained doorway. She pointed just inside. "Stand here." Then she slipped through the hanging fabric and said, "Mr. Reddick, may I present your bride?"

She pulled a cord, and the curtains parted, leaving Adina exposed to his view.

Coughing on a gulp of tea, Kirk set the cup aside and stood. "Adina, you look like a goddess. Never have I seen a woman more beautiful."

She walked into the room, unable to believe she could

look that good. "Do you mean that, or are you joshing me?"

"Joshing? Never." He walked around her, making humming noises in his throat. "I'm flabbergasted. You were beautiful to me before, but this shows me how gorgeous you can be." He stopped in front of her and took her hands. "Are you sure you want to marry me? You could capture the heart of a king."

She laughed nervously. "Don't be ridiculous. I've never known a more caring, intelligent, handsome man. Of course, I want to marry you. You're a king to me.

Kirk glanced at Glory, who stood by the curtain, smiling. "Tell her I'm not being ridiculous, Glory."

"He's right, Adina." Glory walked up to her and took hold of her arms. "You are stunning in this outfit. You're walking to the church, right?"

She nodded.

"Notice the stares you get from the people you pass, especially the men. They won't believe their eyes." Glory flashed a grin at Kirk. "You are right about one thing, Adina. You won't find a nicer, more gentlemanly man to marry, and he's also handsome. You're lucky to have found each other. Tell me, Kirk, do you have a brother by any chance?"

He laughed. "I do, but he's only twenty. You need

someone more mature, worldly, and perhaps wealthier."

She made a disappointed face, then smiled. "I'll just have to keep looking then."

Adina stepped over and took Glory's hands. "Thank you for everything. You've been so sweet to me. I feel you're a friend now, and I'm so grateful for finding you and all you did for me."

Glory drew her into a quick embrace. "I feel the same way. I hope you and Kirk settle here so we can see each other often."

"That sounds fabulous, but his job requires him to travel a lot, so I'm not sure that can happen, at least not yet. We're hoping for a change that might happen soon."

"I'll hope for that, too, then. The women my age here are married or work at bordellos, so I could use a friend. The wedding is going to be soon, right?"

Adina nodded. "We'll be heading for the church when we leave here."

"Do you have someone to stand up with you?"

"The preacher said he'd probably find someone, his wife, and someone else."

Glory's eyes held yearning and uncertainty. "I would love to be that someone else."

"That would be marvelous," Adina exclaimed. "But

what about your shop? You might miss a customer."

Laughing, Glory flapped a hand at that. "So be it. I'll call it my lunch break."

"You are wonderful." Impulsively, Adina grabbed the woman and kissed her cheek.

"Why, thank you. I've become fond of you, too. Shall we go?"

"Yes." Together, they pushed through the curtain.

Kirk rose from the chair where he'd been sitting. "Are you ready?

"I'm very ready," Adina told him. "And guess what, Glory's going to be my maid of honor."

"Perfect. And what a treat for me to escort two such lovely ladies."

The three strolled down the street, Kirk in the middle and up the hill to where the church stood. Inside, they found the preacher waiting with two women, one his age, the other younger.

"Mr. Reddick," the preacher said, "good to see you back. Are you all prepared to be wed to this beautiful young bride? I see she found a dress as attractive as herself."

Kirk glanced at Adina, who smiled back. "Yes, we are both ready. I assume you know Miss..."

"Holcomb," Glory provided.

"I have not had the pleasure, but I know my wife has."

"Hello, Glory," the older of the two women with the preacher said. "I can tell you made the bride's gown. Your designs stand out from all the rest."

"Why, thank you, Helen," Glory answered.

Helen motioned to the girl beside her. "This is our daughter, Ann. She's almost old enough to start shopping at your store."

"I look forward to the opportunity," Glory said.

"Shall we begin?" Pastor Jones asked.

Everyone nodded, and he instructed them where to stand.

Kirk and Adina faced each other in front of the altar. The minister stood behind it. Glory and Ann stood to Adina's left, Helen to Kirk's right. After a brief prayer, the pastor spoke a few words about the seriousness of the rite the bride and groom were about to swear to and the joy they could achieve by caring for each other with love and respect.

"Kirk Reddick, do you take this woman, Adina Kinnaird, to be your lawfully wedded wife, to love, honor, and support?"

Kirk peered into Adina's eyes as he replied, "I do."

"Adina Kinnaird, do you take Kirk Reddick as your

lawfully wedded husband to love, honor, and obey?"

"I do."

"Then, by the powers invested in me by God and the town of Silver City, I pronounce you man and wife," he announced. "Kirk, you may kiss your bride."

"Gladly," he said and drew Adina into his arms. The kiss went too quickly for the bride and groom but not for those who watched.

When they broke apart, everyone congratulated them and wished them a good, happy life.

Adina said a private, silent prayer that she would not disappoint Kirk and that all went well for them.

Kirk dropped money into a collections plate on the altar and took out his watch. "Four o'clock. Close enough to suppertime, and I'm buying for anyone who wishes to join us at the Idaho Hotel restaurant."

"I regret that I and my family have a funeral to attend in a short time," Pastor Jones said and thanked them.

"I'd love to come," Glory said, "but I think I'd best return to my shop. Adina, please drop by before you leave town, okay?"

"Yes, I will. Again, thank you for everything."

"It was a true pleasure." Glory leaned in and kissed Adina's cheek, whispering, "Be happy."

"I believe I will be," she whispered back.

They said their goodbyes and headed for the hotel. Glory walked with them but stopped at the entrance to return to her store.

Adina felt both regret and appreciation toward the shop woman. She looked forward to dining with her new husband but was still nervous about the night. Mrs. Kirk Reddick. Adina Reddick. She felt strangely the same, yet different. Glancing at the ring Kirk had slipped onto her finger during the ceremony, she wondered when he'd purchased it. It was gorgeous, with a ruby in the center, bracketed by tiny diamonds, and with scrolls engraved on the band.

"Look inside," he said.

She slid the ring off and read the inscription: For My Forever Bride, July 13, 1878.

"Oh, that's sweet, Kirk." Leaning in, she kissed him.

"Don't get me started on kisses, or I won't be able to stop," he said.

She laughed nervously, then cleared her throat. "Kirk, would you be terribly disappointed if we waited until we get back from Flint to...you know..."

"To consummate our marriage?" he finished for her.

She nodded. Did he sound disappointed? She thought

he did and felt guilty for it.

He took hold of her arms and peered into her eyes as if to make sure she heard him. "Adina, we will wait until you feel ready to begin conjugal relations. All right? We both need time to get to know each other. When the time is right, we'll know it."

"Thank you. I know I'm going to love being your wife. I just feel...I don't know. A little shy, I guess."

"That's understandable. Matters have moved unusually fast for us. There's no need to be in a rush. When you're ready will be soon enough. We don't even need to share a bed. Even after we get our new wagon, we'll still have Russ's tent."

"It's no wonder I'm falling in love with you," she said, kissing his cheek. She had seen disappointment in his eyes before he spoke.

"I feel the same about you. Still want to eat?"

"Yes."

He showed her the menu. "They're serving beef ribs tonight with a special sauce, the menu posted outside the door said. It sounds good, doesn't it?"

"Sure does. Let's see if they're serving yet."

"Yes. Maybe afterward, we can stop by the marshal's office and see if he had any luck finding that man who killed Jason."

"Good idea." They pushed through the door and found a table. Having learned of their wedding, the owner brought out a white sheet cake for dessert with their names spelled out in mint-flavored green frosting. Kirk invited everyone present to take a piece. When they left, they took Glory a piece, then went to the jail.

Unfortunately, the marshal wasn't in.

"I'm afraid I have bad news for you, folks," said the gangly deputy, George, who looked far too young to be a lawman.

"What is it?" Kirk asked.

Adina had a bad feeling in her stomach, and it wasn't a tummy ache. It was fear.

"The marshal was found dead two miles out of town this morning with a bullet in his back," the deputy said.

Feeling faint, Adina dropped onto a chair. Kirk laid a comforting hand on her shoulder.

"Are you all right?" he asked, peering at her.

"I'm fine," she said. "It's the marshal who's dead, and we both know who did it."

"You know?" George asked. "Who?"

"A man registered at the hotel as Sam Smith," Kirk told him. "He reserved room ten through tomorrow, but I bet he never returns."

"No," Adina said. "He'll be looking for me now."

Chapter Eight

Leaving Silver City, Kirk decided to take a back road into Flint, which he'd learned about from the clerk at the Idaho Hotel. It allowed him to avoid running into the men they'd met before reaching Silver City, who'd hoped to stop him from reaching Flint. They'd surely miss him if they were looking for a wagon. But he rode a horse instead, rented from the livery. The rough trail took extra time to reach his destination, but he had no problems.

He wondered how angry Adina was to find him gone. He felt guilty for leaving her behind but had to keep her safe. He'd arranged with Deputy George to keep an eye on her and watch for Sam Smith. George had orders not to let a single man he didn't know come near Adina. The town had elected an older deputy, Erwin, to be the new marshal. It pleased Kirk because it left George free to give Adina all his attention. Because of the marshal's murder, the town hired two other deputies.

Kirk prayed she didn't become angry enough to have their marriage annulled while he was gone. He knew little about love, but he suspected that was what he felt for her. In truth, he had few doubts.

He'd left a note for Glory at her shop, asking her to do what she could to smooth things with Adina and keep his wife too busy to stay mad at him until he returned. He could only hope it worked.

Flint resembled every other small mining boom town, with the usual businesses lining the street. One feature he assumed temporary was a gallows with two nooses hanging from the crossbar. This one was wide open, unlike the one at Red River Crossing, so everyone could see the corpse hanging, no matter where they stood.

Kirk checked in with the town marshal first. The lawman was alone, which was good. He assumed the prisoners he was to hang were in a cell in the backroom and was glad not to see them. The marshal was a squatty, overweight man in overalls with a nose that suited him since it resembled a pig's snout. An open sack of donuts sat on his desk, and a bit of chocolate frosting showed at the corner of his mouth when he greeted Kirk. "Howdy. I'm Marshal Hurst. What can I do for you, stranger?"

Kirk introduced himself.

The marshal stood and held out a hand. "Glad to meet ya, Reddick. Got two men for ya to string up. Held up the bank and shot a teller and one of my deputies."

"Very well. I'll tell you now that I don't want anyone to know who I am, and I'm counting on you to help see that no one finds out. For the hanging, I'll wear a hood with only eyeholes. I'll leave my horse behind the building nearest to the gallows to have it available immediately after. I won't hang around."

The marshal stuck his thumbs inside his waistband. "Well, now, that ain't too friendly. I figured on having a drink with ya after the hanging."

"I appreciate the thought, Marshal, but...is this your first hanging?"

"Yep, shore is."

"Well, you'll find out tomorrow that folks don't like hangmen much. They usually throw rotten fruit and vegetables at me, and sometimes they shoot at me." He removed his hat and pointed to the still-red scar from Red River Crossing. "I received this at a recent such event."

"I'm plumb sorry to hear that, Reddick. Makes a man wonder why you took the job."

Kirk sighed. He hated repeating this story. "Let's just say that a judge appointed me, and it's not something I could get out of, or I wouldn't be here."

"Appointed, huh?" Hurst said.

"That's right."

"As a punishment? What'd ya do, steal his sweetheart?" Hurst chuckled.

"No, to both. Can I count on you not to reveal who I am to anyone in this town, where I am at any given time, or what direction I take after the hanging's over?"

"Reckon so. Don't want ya getting shot in my town." He grinned. "Though I can't imagine there's much chance o' that. Folks here are right friendly."

"That's what I was told at my last job. You might keep an eye out for a group of strangers who'll try to enflame the people to cause trouble. I've seen it happen in a few towns. No one's been able to identify or catch them. Nor do I know why they do it, except they hate hangmen."

Hurst latched onto his overall bib straps and puffed out his chest. "Wal, if they pull their tricks here, they'll find out their time is up 'cause they won't get away from me."

Sure. Kirk nodded and left for the hotel. He'd arrange

to have his meals brought to the room, study the town to figure out the best way to get to the gallows, and then try to concentrate on the book he brought with him. He'd been reading it when he arrived in Red River Crossing and hadn't had much time to give to it since.

The following day, after eating breakfast in his room, Kirk dressed in his black outfit and pulled on the new hood Adina had sewed for him by hand. She'd done a good job, and his head had healed enough now that it wouldn't bother him to wear it. It had remained sore in De Lamar. He exited the hotel by the back entrance, picked up his horse, which the stable boy had saddled for him as arranged, then rode down a back road until he came to an alley he knew would put him where he needed to leave the horse.

No sooner had he reached the stairs to the top of the gallows than a man approached him, a grubby stick of a man who looked like a snake and probably was one. "You the hangman?"

There seemed no reason to deny it. He wore his disguise, which made him stick out like a broken nose with a black eye. He held himself still, ignoring the panic building inside him. Something was wrong. He felt it as if a thunderbolt had struck him. "Yes. What do you want?"

"Got a message for ya from yer wife."

He started to say he didn't have a wife, then his heart fell. Adina. She would never use a lowlife like this to bring him a message. Something was wrong here. He was about to demand to know what was going on when the marshal arrived.

"What are you doing here, Cactus Pete? You pestering the hangman?"

"Just got an important note for him, is all."

Kirk lifted a hand to stall the marshal, then held his palm out to Cactus Pete. "Give it to me."

Pete handed it over. Kirk unfolded the grimy piece of paper and read, *Kirk, I'm being held by these men. If you go through with the hanging, they'll kill me.*

"What the...?" He grabbed the man, dropping the paper scrap, and yanked him close. "Where is she? You take me to her, or I'll put you in a noose and hang you."

With a grunt, the marshal bent over and picked up the note.

"Hold on here." Hurst took hold of Kirk and inserted himself into the conversation with the filthy messenger. "How do we know you have his woman?"

"Oh, yeah." Pete dug in his pocket and held out a dirty hand, the fingernails black with dirt. "I was 'sposed to give ya this."

Kirk snatched it from him: Adina's locket—the one with her parents' pictures that she'd offered him to prove he could trust her. He shoved it in his pocket. As fear tightened his nerves and heightened his pulse, he swallowed hard. She was in trouble. He never should have left her alone in Silver City. She'd have been safer with him. Now, he was in a devil of a situation.

Stepping a few feet over to where Marshal Hurst stood, he said, "You're going to have to keep the prisoners a little longer. My wife needs me."

"So I see." Hurst tossed the note aside. "I'll get some men and—"

"No," Kirk said. "I'm going alone. A posse would scare them, and who knows what they'd do to Adina then."

"We're talking about the Pierce gang. I need to capture them, Reddick."

Kirk glanced around. People were showing up for the hanging, but luckily, none were nearby. Leaning close to the marshal, he said, "I told you not to use my name. I'm trusting you with my life, Hurst. And now my wife's, as well. Watch what you say."

"All right. All right. But let me get a few men to go with you."

"I said no." He turned back to Pete. "I'll get my horse. Meet me behind the jail."

Pete jabbed a finger at Hurst. "You follow us, and you'll be spotted and shot down before you ever get close to our hideout."

Kirk felt the marshal's angry eyes on his back as he and Cactus Pete raced off in opposite directions. Kirk swung into his saddle and waited only moments before Pete rode up.

"You have any weapons hidden anywhere on you?" he asked.

"I left my gun belt and pistols in my room."

"Good." Pete waved for him to follow and headed out of town.

Kirk's mind whirled with questions: how had they gotten Adina? Where were they, and had they hurt her? How would he rescue her? He couldn't give them what they wanted. The law demanded those men hang for their crimes. If he didn't do it, the judge would have to call in another hangman or move the prisoners, but it would happen.

The judge would be unhappy. Could this end their deal and Cage's freedom? Kirk had to find an answer to keep his brother and Adina safe. He would have to judge the situation when they reached the gang, and he could better see what he was dealing with.

He followed Cactus Pete for at least half an hour through rough sagebrush terrain where pine saplings struggled to grow among tree stumps on otherwise denuded land, thanks to the old mines in the area. At least he had a good view of everything—until they descended into a dry gully gouged out of the earth by a stream in flood sometime in the past and now long gone. The ravine wound for a hundred yards before widening into a perfect hiding place for outlaws. The ravine's sides rounded up and formed a thick lip that hid the men waiting below. A dense growth of saplings along the rim made it impossible for lawmen to sneak up on them. Anyone wishing to enter had to come up the gorge like he and Cactus Pete, where they would be spotted and no doubt shot. A half dozen men stood or sat around a fire drinking coffee. Horses lined the opposite side.

Kirk searched for Adina, finding her tied up and sitting against the wall. He leaped off his horse and hurried to her. "Are you all right?"

"She's fine." An older man he assumed to be the gang leader rose and approached. He had a head like an upside-down pear with a glob stuck on for a nose and a belly that hung over his belt. "Did you bring any cash?"

"No one told me I needed to. I have about thirty dollars." Kirk lied. He had two hundred in his boot but handed him the thirty.

Kneeling beside Adina, Kirk slicked a hand over her tangled hair, licked his thumb, and used it to remove some of the dirt on her face. She looked so scared; he wanted to bundle her in his arms and carry her out of there. "Are you okay?"

"For the most part, but I'm sure they'll kill us before this is over. Can you stop the hanging?"

"All I can do is refuse to do it, but the marshal won't release them. He'll wire the judge and ask what to do. John—the judge—will send another hangman to do the job."

"That's too bad," Pear-head said. "I hate to kill you both for nothing. 'Course, the woman can entertain the men before she has to go."

"You touch her, and I'll find a way to kill you."

"Not if you're dead. Turn around, hangman," the boss man ordered.

Kirk guessed what was coming. Sure enough, he tied Kirk's hands behind his back and told him to sit by Adina and keep quiet. He also gagged Adina so she could not say another word.

Once Pear-head returned to his men at the fire, Kirk

whispered, "Nod if you're really okay, Adina."

She nodded.

"We must figure out a plan. I wish you didn't have that gag so we could talk. I'm hoping the marshal will have followed or maybe tracked us."

Over at the fire, someone must have cracked a joke because they broke into raucous laughter. Kirk wished he could have some of the coffee they were drinking. He hadn't had anything since breakfast, and it was mid-afternoon.

"Have they fed you?" he asked.

She shook her head.

"I was afraid of that. Who knows if they'll feed us when they eat? I see one chewing jerky. I could settle for that."

A muffled sound came from her, and he saw her working her gag down from her mouth. "I can't tell you how glad I am to see you. Thank you for coming after me."

"Of course. You're my wife. I care about you. If we turned back to back, we could try to untie each other."

"Why not? They'll kill us eventually anyway."

"At least we have a plan. That gives us part of a chance." He scooted his bottom around as he spoke so his back was to her. He heard the scuffling as she did the same and soon felt her hands searching for his. Her slender fingers were nimbler but didn't have the strength of Kirk's.

Even so, she managed to free him first.

"Good job," Kirk praised her. "I can work faster on yours now. Watch and warn me if they look over."

"They're cooking, drinking, and ignoring us."

"All the better for us."

She shook her hands when the rope fell away to get the feeling back into them. Kirk helped by massaging her wrists. "Better face forward again and keep our hands behind us so they think we're still tied up.

"What do we do if they bring food and go to untie us?" Adina whispered.

"Throw it in their faces and run for the horses. They haven't unsaddled mine or Pete's."

"All the better for us," she repeated his earlier words.

"Let's pray nothing changes before we can escape." True to his nature and his chosen occupation, he bowed his head.

Adina did as well. She made up her own since she couldn't hear Kirk's prayer. Two might improve their chances.

Eventually, one they heard called Switchblade approached with a tin plate of what looked like stew. Adina cast a fearful glance at Kirk. She wasn't sure she dared to throw hot food in the man's face. He set the plate down and removed her gag. She tensed, ready to act, but instead of untying her hands, he filled a spoon with meat and told her to open her mouth. When she did, he shoved it in. While she chewed, he fed Kirk, then her, until the plate was empty. She would have liked more, but the man returned to the fire and sat to eat his meal. He didn't bother to replace her gag.

When the food was gone, they got out bedrolls and laid them around the fire. They ignored Kirk and Adina, who felt quite cold. When she began to shiver, she whispered, "I'm freezing."

"Try scooting closer to me," Kirk said. "That's all we can do for now. Once they fall asleep, we'll grab our chance."

"What if I distract them while you escape and go for the marshal? I could do a gypsy dance. I saw one once on a stage, and I think I could imitate it."

"You mean swirling your skirt around and giving them glimpses of your legs?" he asked. "That would distract them all right until they became so aroused they threw you down and had their way with you. Are you crazy?"

"It was just an idea." She shut up, not having any other notions. It made her feel good, though, that he couldn't bear the idea of her being violated. It meant he cared for her, maybe a lot.

Chapter Nine

Everything happened so fast that Adina couldn't precisely say what happened during the next hour. The gang was asleep, and she and Kirk were about to mount their horses to escape when the marshal called out from the edge of the camp, "This is Marshal Hurst from Flint. You're surrounded. Stand up and toss your weapons toward the fire, or you'll be shot."

Kirk grabbed Adina, threw her on the ground, covered her with his body, and told her to be still.

Men jumped out of bed and fired into the dark. A barrage of bullets came from the perimeter of the camp, mowing the outlaws down like trees before an avalanche.

When it was over, the marshal and several others entered the camp and began checking bodies.

"Heavens, Kirk," Adina said. "They killed them all."

"Hurst doesn't believe in taking men alive. If they're outlaws, they need to be killed, according to him. It's a bit brutal, in my opinion. I've known men who'd been outlaws but saw the light and changed their ways. Every man deserves a second chance, I think."

"I agree. Hurst is almost as bad as the outlaws in a way."

He helped her to her feet. The marshal saw them and swaggered over. "Well, you don't need to worry about them anymore." He glanced at the bodies piled up near the fire. Men lit torches to ensure they'd gotten all the outlaws. A deputy fetched horses and began loading bodies to carry them to town. A few men remained alive, though wounded.

"There are a few bounties to be collected," Hurst said, watching the goings on. "I figured I'd give the money to you since we wouldn't have gotten the gang if not for you two."

"I wouldn't feel right accepting any such money, Marshal. We did nothing to capture this gang, and—"

"I'll take it," Adina said quickly, grabbing Kirk's arm and squeezing it. She looked up at him, an earnest look in her eyes. "This could give us a new start, Kirk. If we don't take it, someone else will. And if I hadn't tried to come after you, the gang wouldn't have captured me and used me to try to stop the hangings, so in a way, we did help catch them."

"It's bloodied money, Adina. How could your conscience—"

"She's right, Reddick," Hurst butted in. "If you don't want the bounty, I'll give it to someone in town. As a lawman, I can't take it, but I'd hate to see it go to waste, and you deserve it more than anyone else."

Kirk decided to shut up. If Adina wanted the money, he'd let her have it. Maybe she and the marshal were right. He had plenty of money in the bank, thanks to his inheritance from his grandparents, but she didn't know that yet, and he wasn't about to tell her in front of Hurst.

After the marshal walked away, Adina moved in front of Kirk, forcing him to look at her. "This county took part of your life away from you by forcing you to be a hangman instead of what God intended you to be: a preacher. This money is a small payback for what you've lost, being unable to earn your living properly. Where do you get the money for your expenses, Kirk?"

"I get a stipend from the county," he said. She would

make an excellent, protective mother someday.

"And you never have to dip into your own pocket?"

He tried to turn away, but she stepped before him again. "Do you, Kirk?"

"Yes," he growled. "I've had to use some of my savings. So what?"

"So what?" she mimicked, waving her arms. "Why must you be so stubborn? You deserve this money. Being the hangman is an ugly, thankless job. To be required to live off your savings is a sin. The least the county can do is see to your financial needs without you having to pay your own way. You earned this cash, and I aim to see you accept it, or I'm done with this whole charade."

He stared off into the distance, saying nothing.

Tears rolled down Adina's cheeks as her heart shattered. She turned to the marshal. "Sir, can you tell me where to go to catch a stagecoach to Red River Crossing?"

He glanced at Kirk and back at her. "Ain't you two married?"

"Yes and no," she said. "I can't be married to a man too proud and stubborn to take what is owed him. I guess you'll have to give the money to someone else."

"Very well. The stage stop is in the Wells Fargo office a few doors down from the jail," Hurst said. "You can't miss it."

"Thank you." Throughout her exchange with the marshal, Kirk remained turned away from her. She climbed onto her horse. "Is there someone who can escort me to town? I don't want to get lost."

"Sure." The marshal glanced between her and Kirk again, then yelled for one of his deputies. "Rodney, take this lady to town, will you?"

A tall young man with light hair and deep blue eyes came and led her mare behind some boulders beyond the gully where the posse had left their horses. There, he mounted up, and they rode away.

Adina wanted to look at Kirk and plead with him not to let her go, but pride wouldn't allow it. In the same way, pride wouldn't let him accept the money, she supposed. But she was right. He deserved that reward. The county had used him, used his brother's misfortune, and wouldn't even pay his expenses. It was wrong.

Was she wrong for trying to make him take it?

That question would haunt her clear to town and then to Silver City, where she collected her belongings. She returned her wedding dress to the shop and told Glory what happened.

"But, Adina," she argued, "you two are perfect for each

other, and I could see how much you love him. He loves you, too. Was the money that important?"

Adina looked at her friend and asked herself the same question. "I don't know, Glory." She sat on a stool and stared at the dress Glory held, the beautiful gown she was married in. "Am I wrong? Why wouldn't he take it? The marshal would give that money to someone; why shouldn't it be Kirk? No one deserved it more."

Frustration had her jumping up and pacing the floor while Glory watched with confusion on her lovely face.

"I hate stubbornness," Adina said. "Oh, I can see there are times when it's the right thing when it means someone will suffer if you give in. But who would have suffered if Kirk had taken that money? His pride? Why? How could it damage his pride? He'd been wronged, and the county owed him for it. That judge who allowed Kirk to assume his brother's sentence thought Cage innocent. Why hadn't he simply let him go? Doesn't a judge have that right?"

Helplessly, she looked to Glory for an answer, but her friend merely shrugged.

"I don't know, Adina. I know nothing of the law or how it works. But I have to say that it sounds logical to me that the judge should have let Kirk's brother go. Could have let him go free." Glory suspended the dress from a hook. "The question, though, is why Kirk wouldn't take the money and why it's so important to you that you'd leave him for it."

Adina frowned as she stared at Glory. "You think I'm wrong."

"I think you're crazy. Adina, the man loves you. You love him. Why let this money come between you?"

"Maybe you're right." To help keep from bawling, Adina began picking at her fingernails. "It doesn't matter now. He let me leave and didn't come after me. Does that seem to you like he's in love with me?"

With a sad expression, Glory put the kettle on for tea. "I don't know what to tell you, Adina. But if he feels he's right, he isn't likely to come after you. A man's pride is a monstrous thing. To ignore it would be like surrendering himself to an enemy. A man who does that is too often a broken man with nothing left to live for."

Adina felt as if a blade had been thrust through her heart. Tears filled her eyes. "Oh, Glory, is that what I've done to Kirk? I love him. How could I have done that? I had no right to try to force him to make that choice." She spun toward the door. "I've got to find him."

"Wait, Adina," Glory followed her. "I forgot to tell you a man was in here yesterday asking about you."

Adina froze. "What man?"

"He was tall and nice-looking but had the coldest blue eyes I've ever seen."

"Was he blond and young?"

"Yes."

Adina sank against the wall next to the door as if she couldn't hold herself up. Her muscles had gone slack, and she felt woozy like she might faint. "I need to sit down."

Glory lurched forward to grab her before she could fall and helped her to a chair. Crouching beside her, she asked, "What is it, Adina? Who is this man?"

"He's a killer. He murdered my boss in Red River Crossing, and he wants me dead because I saw him. What am I going to do, Glory?"

"You're going to stay right here." Glory rose, drawing Adina up with her, and hauled her into the back, pushing her onto a divan. "Sit here, or lie down, while I find the marshal. I'll lock up and hang the closed sign. Don't go anywhere and stay away from the windows."

Glory hurried out then.

Adina lay on the divan, wondering where Kirk was. Would he come back to Silver City? Would he look for her? What about the wagon they were having built for them? And where was the killer, Sam Smith, as he called himself when he checked into the hotel? It certainly wasn't his real name. Did he know about Kirk? Would Kirk recognize him? What if they ran into each other, and he shot Kirk?

She sat up as fear gripped her heart. She had to find Kirk and keep him safe somehow. New strength filled her as she ran into the other room and tried the door. Glory had locked it from the outside. She couldn't open it.

Scanning the street, she saw a black horse with a red saddle blanket outside the hotel. Sam Smith was here somewhere.

A rider entered the town from the direction of Flint. Adina watched until he came close enough to identify.

It was Kirk.

Please, come here, Kirk. Don't go to the hotel.

He rode up to the hotel, dismounted, and went inside.

Worried and heartbroken, Adina sat down and put her head in her hands. Where was Glory? Why hadn't she returned? Adina needed to get out of there.

Hearing a loud thud from the other room, she jumped up. Before she could do anything else, Sam Smith appeared in the curtained doorway between the shop and Glory's working area.

"So, I finally found you," he said. "You know who I am?"

"Would it work for me to deny it?" She edged toward

the door even though she knew it to be locked.

"Oh, I know you saw me," he said, "and I got a good look at you. I'd know you even if you changed your hair." He walked closer and reached to touch the strands that fell to curl beside her face. She flinched away. "It's real pretty hair. You're a beautiful woman. I hate like hell that I must kill you, but you know I have no choice. I don't think I'd like prison."

"What if I promise not to tell on you, even if they catch you and put you on trial? I could lie and say I don't recognize you."

He chuckled. "You think I'd trust you to do that? Do I look stupid?"

"No, I'd think you're too smart to embroil yourself in this situation. Why did you kill Jason?"

"Because he was going to expose me in his paper."

"Expose you for what?"

"Are you hoping if you keep me talking long enough, your friend will return and save you? You think I'd let that happen?"

"She went for the marshal."

"Is that so?" He stepped to the window and looked out. "Yep. I see them coming now. Guess we're going out the rear door that I kicked in."

Taking her firmly by the arm, he dragged her toward the back room. Adina dug in her heels and resisted for all she was worth, even grabbing the counter with her free hand so he couldn't pull her away, but he was stronger than her, and she had to let go. She did manage to overturn a basket of thread in the process. She grabbed hold of a spool and hid it in her palm. She allowed the thread to unroll as they passed through the curtain, leaving a nearly invisible trail behind them.

"How are you going to get your horse?" she asked, hoping to slow him down. "It's at the hotel."

"It's too easy to spot," he said. "I had to find another one."

By then, they were outside, and she saw two horses waiting. Blast, he was way ahead of her. But she knew what was coming next and decided to fight him.

When he went to lift her into the saddle, she kicked him between the legs. He let go, grabbing his privates and cursing violently.

Adina took off running for her life and screaming for help.

She didn't get far before he had her again and struck her hard.

KIRK

Kirk stared from Gloria to the marshal and back as they stood in the hotel lobby where Gloria had found the two men. "What do you mean the killer has Adina?"

"She told me about the man who shot her employer in Red River Crossing," Gloria said. "I told her about a man who came to my shop asking about her, and when I described him, she said he was the same man. That's when I went to get the marshal, but when we reached the shop, she was gone, and the back door had been kicked in."

"I saw sign of two horses having been in the alley," the marshal said. "It looks like he headed south out of town."

Kirk swore under his breath. Why had he argued with her? If they'd returned together, this wouldn't have happened. He shouldn't have let her go. So what if he took the bounty from those outlaws? She was correct; he'd earned it. Now she was gone, and that murderer would kill her the first chance he had. "We have to go after him right now."

He headed for the door.

"I'll get a posse," the marshal said.

"I'm not waiting. You can catch up."

He exited the hotel and went straight to his horse, followed by the marshal and Glory. The black gelding with the white face Adina had told him belonged to the killer still stood at the hitching post. "He's abandoned his horse, probably because it's too easy to identify. The saddlebags are gone, though."

As he spoke, he swung into the saddle, backed away from the hitching post, turned the horse, and got him going. Riding behind the stores, he dismounted and crouched to examine the horse prints outside Glory's shop. As he was about to rise, discouraged at not finding anything to help him, he saw a thread leading away from the tracks. Curiously, he picked it up and followed it out of the alley toward the main street.

The thread was no accident, he decided. Adina probably grabbed it as she was hauled from the store and reeled it out as they rode along, like leaving a breadcrumb trail. He mounted up and, keeping hold of the thread, followed it out of town a couple of miles until he came to a side road. A sign read, *Waste Disposal*. The thread turned and went down that road.

The killer probably intended to kill Adina and hide her body in the town's trash. Kirk was about to kick his horse into action when he heard riders coming from the direction of Silver City. The marshal, probably. He decided to wait another minute or two. He was about to give up and leave when the posse caught up to him.

The marshal drew up alongside. "Have you learned anything?"

"Yeah, I found a thread and followed it to this turn-off. I figure Adina took the thread with her and is letting it out as they go along. He'll plan on killing Adina and hiding her in the trash."

Marshal Green turned to his men. "Spread out, circle around to the dump, and close in cautiously so you're not seen. We want to get this murdering piece of horse manure alive if we can. Kirk and I will ride more directly in and try to take him by surprise. Your job is to make sure he doesn't escape and to keep him from killing the girl."

The men took off, and Kirk and the marshal continued up the narrow road. When it curved, and the stench from the dump became overpowering, the marshal stopped. "It's just around this corner. We should leave the horses here and go in on foot."

"Good idea." Kirk dismounted and checked his gun.

Green did likewise. Then they separated. Kirk ran closer, keeping his head down and using the hilly terrain and trees as cover.

He spotted Sam Smith almost immediately. Adina, bless her, fought when Smith tried to get her off her horse. She shoved him away with her boot, then kicked the horse to get going, but the killer had the reins and kept her in place. Rebelling against his harsh treatment, the horse danced around, making it difficult for Smith to hang onto him.

Meanwhile, Kirk crept as close as possible. He waved his arms from the top of a rise until Adina saw him and went still. Unfortunately, that allowed the killer to haul her off the horse. She crumpled to the ground as if unable to walk.

From where Kirk hid, he heard the man swearing at her. She argued back until he struck her across the face.

Furious, Kirk rose and ran a few yards closer. "Stop where you are, mister, and let go of her."

Sam Smith, or whatever his name was, looked at him over his shoulder, then dragged her in front of him. "You want to shoot, be my guest."

"I don't need to. You're surrounded by the marshal and his posse. I'd advise you to drop your gun and step away from her before someone gets an itchy trigger finger."

As the killer whirled to glance around him, the men from the posse showed themselves, all with rifles and six guns pointed at Smith. Marshal Green appeared several yards from Kirk. "You heard him. Drop the weapon."

Smith laughed, but it had a nervous ring. "You try shooting me, you're likely to get her. You willing to risk that?"

"You think you can just walk out of here?" Kirk asked him.

"Yeah, if I keep her with me."

"You'll need your horse to get very far." Kirk inched closer. "How will you mount up and keep her between you and all these guns?"

Smith didn't reply. He had Adina facing away from him, one arm encircling her neck. Suddenly, she clamped down on his bare wrist with her teeth and kicked back at his shin at the same time. Yelping, he tried to step out of reach of her sharp heel and free his arm from her mouth.

Taking advantage, Kirk darted the remaining yards between them and stuck his Colt in the man's back. "Drop it and release her, or I'll squeeze this trigger with a great deal of pleasure."

Smith tossed his six-shooter away and let go of Adina. She threw herself into Kirk's arms as the marshal walked up to take over.

"Kirk," she wailed. "I'm so sorry. Forgive me. I shouldn't have interfered with that money. It wasn't important. You're what's important. Are you all right?"

"Me?" He chuckled. "You're the one a cold-blooded murderer had hold of."

"Yeah, but he had no idea how to deal with a woman. I knew I could get away from that idiot."

"My lands, but I adore you." He kissed her then, and she kissed him back.

Whistles rose all around them.

Embarrassed, Adina buried her face in his shirt.

Holding her tighter, Kirk nuzzled his nose in her hair. "Now, if we could just find the rat who framed Cage."

She jerked back and looked up at him. "Kirk, I think I know who he is." She turned and watched the marshal marching her old boss's killer toward the jail. "It's him."

"What are you talking about, Adina?"

"Remember I told you I overheard him arguing with Jason?" she asked.

Kirk nodded.

"He said he couldn't allow Jason to print what he'd told him about framing a man for bank robbery."

"Son of a..." Kirk turned toward Smith.

"Wait, Kirk." She stepped in front of him.

"What?"

"You can't just ask him. We need Cage to come and identify him."

Kirk frowned. "But he's in college in St. Louis. He can't come."

"Then we'll find an artist who can draw a likeness of him and send it to Cage. He can identify him by that."

"Yes." Kirk's frown vanished. "Marshal Green, come join us. It's important."

Green came, and Kirk had Adina repeat what she'd told him.

"Sounds like it could be Smith, all right." Green smoothed a hand over his beard.

Adina wore a huge grin. "And I know just the right person to create the likeness we need of him."

Mrs. Jones was more than willing to do the sketch for them. Proving Smith guilty of framing Cage could mean freedom for both him and his brother. Kirk was so excited;

it was all he could do not to kiss Adina in front of the reverend, his wife, and the marshal.

They mailed the drawing off to Cage that day, barely making it to the post office before closing. Then, they returned to the hotel for supper.

"Let's go for a walk after we eat," Adina said. "I want to tell Glory all that's happened."

"Good idea."

They ate steak with fried potatoes, snap beans, and pie for dessert. Adina ordered an extra piece of chocolate pie to take to Glory, and they walked to the store.

"This is the best news I've heard since you two decided to get married," Glory said, pouring wine in three glasses so they could celebrate.

"Yes, it is good." Suddenly, Kirk realized tonight would be their wedding night, the one they'd put off until after he'd taken care of business in Flint. He glanced at her and saw that she'd had the same thought. He tried to put the question foremost on his mind into his gaze.

Adina grinned at him and nodded.

"We need to go, Glory," he said. "We just remembered some unfinished business we must attend to."

She thanked them for sharing their news, and they left the shop.

"Dare we take time for one other stop?" Kirk asked.

"What is it?" she said.

"I'd like to find out how our wagon is coming along."

"Oh, yes." She grabbed his hand and pulled him toward the carpentry shop. "I want to know, too."

No one was in the shop, and they were about to leave when they heard pounding behind the building. Walking around, they gasped with pleasure to see what looked like a fully assembled sheepherder's wagon.

"Oh, Kirk, it's beautiful." She rushed over to smooth a hand over the polished wood of the wagon bed.

Ivan stepped from inside. "Ah, just who I wanted to see. Your new home is almost ready."

"It's gorgeous, Ivan," Adina said. "And it looks done to me."

"I have a few minor touches left to go," he said, "but come inside and see what you think."

They climbed the steps to enter, and Kirk almost joined Adina in a sigh of satisfaction. "It's perfect," she said. "Look at the bed, Kirk. It's big enough for both of us."

"Yes, did you see the stove?" he said.

She turned to look. "How wonderful. I'll love cooking on this. Oh, and a sink with a faucet. How does this work, Ivan?"

He stepped over from the threshold where he'd stood, watching them admire his work. "I installed a flat waterproof box on the roof to collect rainwater. You can turn pipes on at the sink so that the water will flow down."

"You're a genius," Kirk complimented. He was almost speechless; he was so pleased. "You've done a beautiful job and gone above and beyond our expectations,"

Ivan laughed. "That's what I love to hear."

"When can we take it?" Kirk asked.

"Tomorrow morning would be fine. It will give me the time I need to make the final little adjustments I need to do. I tried to figure out how to add a shower, but the best I could come up with..." He stepped down and motioned for them to follow him.

At the back, he pointed to a second faucet on a pipe that struck out about six inches from the top of the wagon. "See the screw at the side of the pipe by the faucet? If you loosen it, you can draw the pipe out about a foot longer. Inside, under the sink, is a showerhead I ordered from New York. They're installing them in all the better hotels and many homes. You screw that onto the end of the faucet, turn the water on, and you have a shower. Of course, you'll be a bit exposed when you use it, but I'm sure you can find places to camp where you'll be alone."

"My heavens, Ivan," Adina said. "You're utterly amazing. When people see this, they'll come flocking to your door asking you to build them wagons. How perfect for traveling."

"She's right." Kirk took the man's hand and shook it. "You've done a masterful job I doubt anyone else has done or could do. Put an ad in the paper, and you'll have to hire a new crew to help you fill all the orders."

Grinning, Ivan nodded. "I already have two orders just from people seeing this here in the yard, and you got a bargain. I'm raising my price."

"You should," Kirk said, "and I'll pay you whatever you're asking."

"No." Ivan shook his head. "A deal is a deal. I won't take more of your money than what we agreed upon. After all, I have you to thank for prompting me to create this one. I learned a lot doing this job, and it will serve me well in the future."

"Well, we're very grateful," Adina said and kissed his cheek.

"Whoa." He chuckled. "Now, I for sure don't need more money."

"We'll see you in the morning." Kirk slipped an arm

around Adina so the young carpenter couldn't decide to latch onto her and keep her. He'd come so close to losing her when Sam Smith had her; he'd realized just how much he loved her. He hoped her feelings for him were as great, but he'd accept what she could give him, confident that love would grow between them as time passed and only become more significant.

"I have an idea," she said as they walked toward the hotel and steered him in a new direction. They arrived at Glory's Needle, and Kirk opened the door for her.

"Glory?"

She appeared in the curtained doorway. "How was the wagon?"

Kirk and Adina exchanged surprised glances.

"How did you know—"

"I saw you head that direction instead of the hotel when you left here," Glory explained.

"Oh, Glory," Adina hopped a little with excitement. "You have to go see it. He did a fabulous job. It's more beautiful than I imagined it could be."

"It genuinely is a wonder," Kirk added.

"We're going to the hotel, but I had an idea. If Kirk gives you some money, will you go to Ivan Kingsman after we're gone and tell him we paid you to create some clothes for his wife?"

"Why, that's a marvelous idea, Adina," Gloria said. "I can print a special card in his name that says it's worth whatever amount you want to spend."

"Great. What do you think, Kirk?" She peered up at her husband.

"I doubt we could have come up with a better idea if we'd spent a year thinking about it. You are a wonder, Adina Reddick."

"Adina Reddick." She grinned. "That's the first time I've heard my new name. I love it."

"As for the money—" Kirk took out his wallet, drew out some bills, and handed them to Glory. "—will this do?"

"It will do wonderfully."

"All right. That works out perfectly. He refused to take more money from us and truly deserves it."

"I can't wait to see this fantastic wagon," Glory said.

"Everyone's going to want one." Adina hugged Kirk's arm. "And now we have a honeymoon to see to."

She blushed slightly, winning laughter from Kirk and Glory.

"We'll see you before we go," Kirk promised before

hauling his blushing bride from the store.

"Are you sure you're ready for this?" he asked as they walked to the hotel.

"Are you?" she countered.

"Honey, I was ready weeks ago."

"Well, I am ready now. Just be patient with me, as I know little about these things."

"I wouldn't expect anything different."

They entered the hotel, climbed the stairs, and went down the hall to his room. He unlocked the door, pocketed the key, then bent and swooped her into his arms. "Welcome to the bridal suite, my sweetheart."

She buried her face in his shirt as he carried her inside and shut the door. A moment later, the door opened, and a masculine hand hung a sign on the knob, *Do not disturb*.

Epilogue

Three Years Later

"Kirk, Cage," Adina called into the parlor, "Supper's ready. Come and get it."

Standing beside her, Glory piled mashed potatoes into a bowl and laughed. "You think they'll hear you over the noise they're making playing cowboys and Indians with Ryder?"

"They'd better if they want to eat." Adina grinned.

Glory put the potatoes on the table and waited, her hand on her rounded belly and her gaze on the parlor doorway.

"Go ahead and sit down," Adina told her, taking her

own seat. "They'll be in soon."

"Cage likes to push my chair in for me," Glory said. "I don't like to discourage his gentlemanly ways. He might stop doing them."

"Hm." Adina stood. "You may be right. Kirk doesn't open doors for me as much as he did when we were first married."

They waited a few minutes before Adina grew impatient and walked to the doorway. In the parlor, Kirk was on his hands and knees, their two-year-old son, Ryder, on his back, yelling, "Git up, horsey. Gotta get the cal...cal...."

"The cavalry, son," Kirk prompted.

"Horsies don't talk," Ryder scolded, smacking his rump with a toy quirt.

Cage sat on the sofa with a child-sized bow and arrow, laughing at the antics of his brother and nephew. Adina smiled. She loved watching her husband and son play together.

Glory joined her, and they grinned at each other, watching their husbands. "When are you going to tell Kirk you're expecting again?"

"Probably tonight when we go to bed." She couldn't resist putting her hand on her own still-flat tummy. "I hope it's a girl this time."

"I'm also hoping for a girl, but I know Cage would like a boy."

As if he heard her, Cage looked up and saw them in the doorway.

"Is supper ready?" he asked, jumping up. "I'm hungry."

That got Ryder's attention. The boy slid off his father's back and ran to his mother. "Me, too, Ma."

She picked him up and went to sit him in his highchair. By the time she turned around, Kirk was there, waiting by her chair, just as Cage slid Glory under the table in her chair and sat next to her.

"Well..." Kirk took his place at the head of the table. "This looks delicious. I love Sunday suppers and fried chicken."

"I know you do." Adina passed him the platter.

"Great sermon today," Glory told Kirk as she helped herself to a serving of mashed potatoes and handed the bowl to her husband. "I love that the rest of the congregation takes it to heart."

He nodded, taking a chicken breast and passing the plate to his brother. "It seemed timely to talk about sin after the robbery today at the Wells Fargo Office. I heard the bank in Flint was hit too yesterday."

"Yes, but those perpetrators have already been caught by Marshal Hurst. I received a wire from the wife of one of them today asking me to represent her husband at trial."

"Will you take the case?" Kirk asked. "He must be guilty."

"Yes, but that doesn't mean I can't get him off."

Adina frowned. "Oh, Cage. You wouldn't really represent an outlaw, would you?"

"I don't know. Depends on the circumstances. The wife says he wasn't with the gang that day."

"Cage is such a good lawyer—" Glory gave her husband a glowing smile, her shoulder nudging his. "—he could get anyone off."

Adina chuckled. "And you aren't the least bit prejudiced, are you?"

Glory scowled at her. "Of course not. You know he's that good."

"Yes, we know it," Kirk said. "Even the governor is aware of Cage's record for winning cases. I spoke with him last week when he was on his tour to get re-elected."

"And, naturally," Adina said, "he brought up the subject, never you."

"Actually, it was him," Kirk said, unperturbed by the accusation.

Few things flustered him these days. He was too happy with his modern home, much of which Ivan Kingsman built, his wife and his darling son, to let matters rattle him. He had become a definite family man, glad to stay home and write sermons, although they did use their "preacher's" wagon to do some traveling for fun now and then. Ivan had remodeled it so that it had a small bed underneath the big bed tucked behind cabinets at each end. Ryder called it his cave and loved it.

Adina smiled at her husband as she ruminated over the changes that had occurred since Sam Smith—his actual name—was convicted of the bank robbery Cage had been wrongly sentenced for and Cage's slate wiped clean as if his conviction never happened.

Kirk had become known as the hanging preacher in the county, and instead of people avoiding attending his church because of that, they flocked to it in droves. He was highly popular for speaking truths too many folks had begun to forget in this modern day and age when amazing things like telephones and electricity were being invented. No one had electricity yet, but everyone expected it soon and couldn't wait. To think of flicking a switch and having light instead of lighting lamps or candles astounded Adina. And she'd heard that Chester A. Arther, the United States

President after Garfield's assassination, was getting a telephone installed. Of course, it was just a rumor, but she liked to think it true.

"Well, Kirk and I are both proud of how Cage has done." She winked at Glory. "I think it's because of how settled he is now that he's married to a good woman—"

"A marriage you instigated," Kirk interrupted.

"—and is about to become a father. And just because I introduced Glory and Cage doesn't mean I *instigated* it. You make it sound like a crime."

Kirk lifted his gaze to the ceiling, then looked at his brother. "Talking Cage into picking up a dress Glory made you isn't exactly *introducing* them. More like an arranged meeting, one I'm not sure Glory knew about ahead of time."

"Oh, I knew." Glory smiled. "And I'm quite grateful to my dear friend for doing it."

"So am I." Cage put his silverware on his empty plate and slipped an arm around his wife. "In fact, I will be eternally grateful to her for it."

Glory kissed his cheek. "Isn't he the sweetest?"

"Oh, you bet." Kirk performed another eyeroll.

Adina laughed. "Say what you will, Kirk, you can't deny you like having Glory for a sister-in-law twice over."

"Who's denying it?" Kirk threw up his arms as if surrendering. "I'm thrilled with it. My wife has never been happier."

"That's true," Adina confessed, and she would be even happier after the child inside her came to join their world.

Kirk lowered his brows as he looked at her. "You're suspiciously happy tonight. Is there something we need to talk about?"

She rose, picked up her empty plate and his, then kissed him on the forehead. "Most definitely, husband dear, and you're going to love it."

Sneak Peek of
Lance-Book 4 in the series

Chapter One

Lance strode down the narrow train aisle, his gun glinting in the late afternoon light. Wide-eyed passengers shrank back, hands raised, their fear thick as smoke in the confined space. "Ladies and gentlemen, my associates will relieve you of your valuables shortly. Please do as they say and no one will get hurt. While I don't want to shoot anyone, my men won't mind a bit."

Women gasped. A few men glared. Most blinked like frightened owls. Taking their valuables did not interest

Lance, but his men considered it gravy. No, his prize was in the freight car. He sneered, picturing Judge Fred Maitland screaming at his Pinkertons over yet another robbery on his railroad.

"Jack," he said over his shoulder, "Let's get to it."

"Right behind you. Boys, you know what to do."

Two men on each car lifting the possessions of the passengers would keep the train busy. Lance and Jack hurried outside to the next car. Not surprisingly, the door was locked, but Lance always tried. Running out of time, he aimed at the doorknob and kicked. Wood splintered as the hinges screamed and the door flung inward.

Gun cocked, Lance rushed in, ready for the rare railroad employee who might want to die for the contents of the safe. Not this time. A mousy-looking old man wearing thick spectacles shot his hands straight toward the ceiling. Squeaking, he jumped back from the safe.

"Open it," Lance commanded as Jack slipped up beside him, eyeing the car for any other employees.

"I don't know the combination."

"Mister, we have to jump off this train in two minutes. That safe'll be open with or without your help."

As if to make the point, Jack hurried over and slid open the large freight door. The rhythmic click-clack of train wheels and the roar of the wind rushed into the car.

He pointed his gun at the old man's head. "Open it or out you go and I'll do it myself."

The railroad employee gulped, debated, and then dropped to his knees. Licking his lips, he spun the dial with shaky hands. Lance stepped over to watch. "How we doing on time?" The horses were tied a mile and a half up past the bridge. They either had to stop the train in time if they could, jump if they had to. They were about to cross the bridge now.

Jack pulled his watch from his pocket. The glass face was cracked but it worked. "I'd say now is about the perfect time."

Lance didn't understand the comment and looked over at him. A sneer curled the man's lip. Something evil played in the lines of his dark, pock-marked face. "Bye, Lance."

What?

Jack fired just as the train lurched.

Fire tore through Lance's side. He spun and stumbled, his breath snatched out of him. The world tilted and dimmed.

Then he was falling...falling. And darkness swallowed him.

Cat Callahan sighed with contentment as she pulled her wagon into her favorite campsite. Her time in Hot Springs had been well spent. "I might even think about buying a wagon, Jules." The sable-and-black Collie whined in agreement and raised her paw. The gurgle of the Animas River was as peaceful as a rocking chair. Cat loved it here among the tall pines that scented the air.

She pulled the brake and petted Jules. "Let's get Buttercup there situated for the night, then I'll rustle up something for dinner."

She climbed down and Jules leaped after her. Out of habit, Cat quickly assessed the canvas draped over the side of the wagon, protecting the wares she couldn't fit inside her peddler's wagon. Everything looked tight and dry and she turned to her horse.

Buttercup, Cat's faithful mare for half a decade now, fluttered her lips. She was ready to be free of the tack and enjoy a good meal. Cat didn't blame her. As she started to unhitch Buttercup, she glanced up through the pines. She could just make out the angles and X's of the train trestle, several hundred yards upstream. Wonder if there will be any trains through this evening? The slow, steady rumble of one coming now answered the question.

She finished freeing Buttercup and led the sorrel down to the creek. As the horse indulged lazily in a cool drink, Cat gazed into the forest. One day, if she ever felt like she could settle down, it might be this very spot—

She frowned. Had she heard a pop? Like gunfire? She listened intently for several more seconds. "You hear something, Jules?"

The dog was lying by the creek, relaxed, almost bored. If she wasn't spooked, Cat had no call to be. Just her imagination. The rush of the water and the rumbling train passing over the trestle could muddle sounds.

Dismissing the sound, she let Buttercup drink for another minute then tugged her head up. "Come on, girl. Let's make camp." The son was about to slip behind the mountain. They might have another hour before dusk.

Pop! Pop!

Cat drew up. Buttercup and Jules did the same. "I know I heard something that time."

More popping followed, from the direction of the train, but on the other side of the river. No arguing that's gunfire. And the train had come to a stop. There was some trouble up there. A robbery?

Chewing her lip, she glanced over at the setting sun and decided. "Buttercup, I'm sorry, but let's move on down the road aways. I don't like this neighborhood."

Whatever the ruckus was, Cat hoped to leave it behind. An hour further on, she pulled up beside Heywood Rustle, plowing his field behind a behemoth of a horse. He yelled whoah and brought the animal to a halt.

"Hey, Heywood, you mind if I camp in a corner of your pasture? There was some trouble up by the railroad tracks. I'd like to stay clear of it. It'll just be for tonight."

"Sure. More than welcome. You can come eat with the missus and me if you're of a mind."

"Thank you, but don't expect me. It's getting late." She'd barely make camp before full dark settled on her. "I'd like to make camp and put my feet up."

"Sure, sure. Suit yourself. Just wanted you to know you're welcome."

"Appreciate it." She smiled her goodbye and drove through the unplowed part of the field to settle her lumbering wagon in amongst some more pines. Heywood had a creek too, but it was a branch of the Animas. Skinny enough she could jump across it, but at least it was water. She relished a bath tonight.

"All right." She pulled the brake. "Let's try this again." She unhitched Buttercup once more and scooped her some oats from the can she kept under her seat. She gave Jules a bowl of jerky giblets, also from a can underneath her seat. She was putting it back in its home when a piece of chipped wood caught her eye. On the corner of the wagon, a few inches above where her head would be.

She climbed up for a better look, poking and prodding the wood. There was something...she poked a little more and worked a piece of lead out.

A bullet.

In all that shooting, one of the bullets had hit her wagon. At first, she was angry. She could have been hit. Or Jules. Or Buttercup. Where would she be without Buttercup? She loved Jules, but Buttercup was the engine of this whole outfit.

But anger did no good, especially with no one to direct it at. And she sure as heck wouldn't go to the law. "Whatever happened back there, I hope it's over." She had no choice but to let it go, and thank the Lord above no one was hurt.

She dropped the peace of lead into her pocket and built a fire. A random bullet had come too close for comfort, but it just went to prove, the Lord could call you home any second. Best be ready. "And I won't ruminate on it, Lord. What's done is done. Thank you for your protection."

Tossing pine straw on the fragile flames, she turned her mind, instead, toward thoughts of the steak she'd bought on her way out of town. And, oh, wouldn't a quick wash in the creek be nice? Then, a fresh night gown. Clean, crisp sheets. My, wasn't she going to sleep well tonight.

Hot Springs had been good to her. The best sales so far this year. No one knew her from Adam's house cat and this far out west, no one would. She had a lot of blessings to count tonight.

Almost humming with contentment, she tossed another piece of wood on the fire and strode to the back of her wagon. Jules was there, sniffing the door, then a slow growl eased out of the dog. Ominous sounding, it made the hair on Cat's neck stand up and her pulse kick up to a gallop.

"What is it, girl?" Hand shaking, she swallowed and reached for the handle. A raccoon? Squirrels? Jules eased back, ready for whatever might leap out. Her body was a tight spring, vibrating with tension. Her growl was so low and intense, Cat could feel it in the ground.

Whatever was in the wagon, Jules did not like it. What

if was a rabid animal? And she'd left her gun inside the wagon.

Well, she couldn't stand here all night. But should she ease the door open or yank it? Cat's fingers wrapped around the hardware. The feel of the metal emboldened her and she snatched it open.

Almost instantly, the barrel of a gun rose from the shadows, a bloody hand clutching it. Jules tensed to lunge, but Cat threw her arm out to stop her. "Down, girl." The menacing, black hole of the gun barrel sent fear slicing through her mind. Was she a breathe away from—?

The gun began to jitter. A man's face, pale, sweaty, ghostly, emerged from the dark. "Don't make...don't make...a sound." His breathy voice faded. The gun slipped from his hand and he fainted back into the darkness.

Books in the Gun for Hire Series

BOOKS IN THE GUNS FOR HIRE SERIES

Creek
Book 1 ~ Linda Broday ~ March 15
Dustin
Book 2 ~ Margaret Tanner ~ March 30
Kirk
Book 3 ~ Charlene Raddon ~ April 15
Lance
Book 4 ~ Heather Blanton ~ April 30
Devon
Book 5 ~ Carra Copelin ~ May 15
Ash
Book 6 ~ Jo-Ann Roberts ~ May 30
Shad
Book 7 ~ Caroline Clemmons ~ June 15
Clint
Book 8 ~ Tracy Garrett ~ June 30
Landon
Book 9 ~ Cheryl Pierson ~ July 15
Luke
Book 10 ~ Winnie Griggs ~ July 30

About the Author

Charlene likes to say she began her fiction career in the third grade when she told the class, during Show and Tell, that a black widow spider came down from the garage roof and bit her (non-existent) little sister to death.

After two years of college as a fine arts major and a divorce, she moved to Utah, planning to wow the world with her watercolor landscapes—until her sister introduced her to romance novels. She never picked up a paint brush again.

Originally published by Kensington in the '90s, Charlene is an Indie author now. She writes Victorian/western historical romance, except for one contemporary fantasy. It's a frog princess story about a man napping beside a pond, who awakens when a frog jumps on his chest. The frog kisses him and *voila!*—he has a naked medieval princess sprawled over him. Charlene has a vivid imagination and a romantic soul.

Please excuse her now. She just heard a husky whisper from one of the dusty, shadowed corners of her office. Someone lurks there, someone long, lanky and lascivious, beckoning to her. She has no intention of playing coy.

Visit Charlene's webpage, charleneraddon.com and sign up for her newsletter.

Her book cover site is silversagebookcovers.com.

If you enjoyed this book, please consider leaving a review on Amazon.com, Bookbub.com and Goodreads.com.

Author Links

Website
charleneraddon.com
Sign up for Charlene's newsletter.

Book Cover Site
silversagebookcovers.com.

Facebook
www.facebook.com/charleneb.raddon

Amazon
www.amazon.com/CharleneRaddon/e/B000APG1P8

Goodreads
www.goodreads.com/author/show/1232154.Charlene_Raddon

Twitter
twitter.com/craddon

Bookbub
www.bookbub.com/profile/charlene-raddon

Also by the Author

Steamy:
Forever Mine
Tender Touch
Taming Jenna
To Have and To Hold
The Scent of Roses
Sensual:
Maisy's Gamble
Sweet novellas:
A Ride Through Time
Sierra's Tumble
Ride for a Bride
Priscilla, The Widows of Wildcat Ridge #1
Thalia, The Widows of Wildcat Ridge #7
Cadence, The Widows of Wildcat Ridge #13
Ophelia, The Widows of Wildcat Ridge #16
Barclay, Bachelors & Babies Book 4
Jared, Bachelors & Babies Book 7
Chase, Bachelors & Babies, Book 12
Velia, Cupids & Cowboys Book 3
Gage (Ridge), Cupids & Cowboys Book 7

Connor, Cupids & Cowboys Book 12
Carrianne's Debacle, Broad Street Boarding House
Lula Mae, Love Train
Dances in Moonlight
The Outlaw and the Sheriff, Outlaw Brides #1
The Outlaw and the Bounty Hunter #2

Paranormal:
A Kiss and a Dare

Short Stories:
Christmas Seduction
The Reckoning (from *The Posse*)

Printed in Dunstable, United Kingdom